# LEGENDS OF LONG BEACH ISLAND

## STIRRING TALES OF GHOSTS, HAUNTED HOUSES, PIRATES, AND MUCH MORE...

D1637297

## by DAVID J. SEIBOLD and CHARLES J. ADAMS III

AUTHORS OF "SHIPWRECKS NEAR BARNEGAT INLET"

LEGENDS OF LONG BEACH ISLAND
by David J. Seibold and Charles J. Adams III

Copyright 1985 by David J. Seibold and Charles J. Adams III

For information, write to:
David J. Seibold
P.O. Box 6411
Wyomissing, PA 19610

ISBN: 978-0-9610008-2-0

2008 Edition

PRINTED IN THE UNITED STATES OF AMERICA

# LEGENDS OF
# LONG BEACH ISLAND

# TABLE OF CONTENTS

# LEGENDS OF LONG BEACH
# FOREWORD
## by
# CHARLES J. ADAMS III

Long Beach Island has an identity crisis.

This slender stretch of sand "six miles at sea" is, no doubt, the summertime host to thousands of visitors who fish its bays and coves and swim or sun on its beaches. To these folks, the island opens its arms of welcome.

But the island is also the home, the roots, of thousands of people who are true to its dunes and charms all year long, all their lives.

To these Long Beach Islanders, this book is dedicated. It is, to be sure, just another in a series of volumes dedicated to the life and the people of this beautiful land. But it deals with the more mysterious and intriguing character of the island. It is a book touching on the supernatural as well as the natural; the mystery as well as the history.

Much of what you are about to read is the product of years, decades and even centuries of amplification. What had its roots in a simple story of fact grew far beyond its proportion to legend. The process is not unlike the "back-yard gossip" network that can take a simple piece of information and, after several retellings, distort the original facts to an unrecognizable caricature of its original details.

While being very dangerous when dealing with vital facts, this is the process by which legends are created. Our minds are full of American legends: Davy Crockett, Daniel Boone, Benjamin Franklin and many more. Where the facts stopped and the legends began is unrecognizable. It is also, arguably, not terribly important, except to the scholar.

Quite simply, if you are not a scholar, and enjoy pure and simple ghost stories, tales of piracy and treachery, and accounts of derring-do, settle back and ready yourself for a glimpse of the darker, and less conspicuous side of life on Long Beach Island.

Charles J. Adams III
Barnegat Light, N.J.
February, 1985

# THE "BARNEGAT PIRATES" AND OTHER TALES OF TREACHERY ON THE SEA AND THE BEACH

What is a pirate? Is it a swashbuckling Errol Flynn engaged in a duel with a British naval officer or a buccaneer from another ship hoisting a "skull and crossbones" pennant on the mainmast? Is a pirate the somehow wretched, yet somehow romantic cutthroat who sailed the seas in search of booty and bounty?

In reality, pirates are all of this and none of this. Certainly the pirates who plundered the shops, ships and citizenry of distant harbors filled· the descriptions more than the Barnegat Pirates. These chaps were a sorry lot, it is said. The dregs of society, the ruthless lot willing to sacrifice their own integrity for the spoils of selfish barbarism, these unfortunates have etched their exploits in the annals of Long Beach.

That there were true "pirates" on Long Beach or on the mainland is a matter for debate. Timeworn tales, and the lay of the land and sea around Barnegat, would point to the very real probability that these picaroons plied their trade hereabouts.

Indeed, there is little doubt that the Jolly Roger flapped in the wind off Long Beach. Lafitte and Kidd likely sailed their vessels within sight of the island. Some say Captain Kidd actually braved the Barnegat Shoals and found refuge, as well as a burial place for treasure, somewhere on the land surrounding the inlet.

There is little recorded history remaining from the time of the alleged "Barnegat Pirates." There are the stories of the thieves who assembled on the shore from Waretown and Barnegat to plunder the wrecks and encampments on the beaches of Barnegat, and there is the name of Rudolf Raven, which turns up often in such accounts.

Raven was the accused leader of the Barnegat Pirates, and the subject of many contemporary newspaper and pulp magazine accounts. Thought to be the organizer of the band of pirates that ravaged the inlet's victims, Raven has taken his place in the dingy chapters of the area's history.

Ship masters and crew members were quick to spread the rumors of the activities of the pirates of Barnegat. So strong was their persuasion that in the mid-nineteenth century, the governor of New Jersey ordered an investigation.

Again, piracy in the classic, swashbuckling mode was not the question. These "pirates" were more ghoulish in their technique, and relied not so much on physical or numerical strengths but on their own cruel cunning and despicable audacity.

The governor's commission was charged with looking into the allegations that certain people on Long Beach Island and the mainland nearby not only ignored the many shipwrecks that took place there, but also waited with a certain level of anticipation until corpses washed ashore and could be stripped of all that was valuable, useful, or resaleable. "Dread deeds of death and depredation upon the unfortunate castaways of the seas," said author Charles E. Averill of these thugs. Not so, said the gentrified commission which issued its report to the governor in short order.

The report maintained that there was no evidence whatsoever of such wretched conduct. Of the sailors' stories, ". . . each and every one of them (is) utterly untrue. There are no inhuman and guilty actors therein to be punished."

All well and good. Explain then, the persistent accounts of these freebooters. Could the stories be mere poppycock? Simply tales told out of school to romanticize, in some bizarre fashion, early life on Long Beach Island?

Every spit of land, every barrier island, every bay, cape and peninsula on America's eastern shore has its legends. One which recurs up and down the coast is also placed at Long Beach Island.

It is a form of piracy hitherto unfathomable to most who associate piracy with the Jolly Roger, Captain Kidd and Errol Flynn. It is the kind of pirate known as the "wrecker."

Variously known as a "wrecker," "mooncusser" or a handful of other sobriquets, this brand of buccaneer was largely a landlubber and more correctly a fiendish thief.

The legend of the "wreckers" takes the form of "mooncussers" on Cape Cod, Massachusetts. The name is of simple derivation. These men (and there is evidence that women, as well, were engaged in the practice) would cuss at the moon on brightly-lit evenings because they could not carry out their misdeeds.

These misdeeds were also very simple, and ingeniously evil. The wreckers waited until a moonless night, perhaps a night with a touch of fog and a tad of a strong breeze. The lights of the ships offshore were visible, as they sailed the busy shipping lanes north and south from New York. These ships tried to cut their sailing time and distance by coasting as close to shore as possible, avoiding any of the navigational hazards that could bring a voyage to an abrupt and tragic halt.

Navigational equipment being unheard of, these captains and navigators sailed by compass, stars and landmarks. At best, the coastal route was perilous. The hundreds of wrecks at Barnegat Shoals alone is testimony to that claim.

The clever wreckers knew of the ships' desires to "cut the corner" around Long Beach Island, and took full advantage of those quests. They recruited their mules, horses or cows and tied a strong lantern to the beasts' neck. Walking steadily up or down the beach, the wrecker served as a nighttime landmark for unwary helmsmen. Believing that what they were seeing toward the shore was the light of another vessel closer in, these sailors would be tricked into thinking that they could wheel their ship closer to the shore, too.

These wreckers positioned themselves so that any ships snared by this trap would smash into the shoals or be caught awash by the incoming waves and be beached.

What followed remains the most inconclusive of all the parts of the wrecker legend. As mentioned earlier, there were some who believed the human victims of the wrecks were waylaid, even murdered, and stripped of all jewelry, money, etc. The more merciless of the variety (mostly on capes and islands north of Long Beach) were said to take their ill-begotten treasure from the victims as they lay dying. Some even may have, upon finding some resistance due to swelling or bloated knuckles, cut fingers off live victims in order to retrieve gold and silver rings.

The wreckers of the New Jersey coast were a bit more humane, it is said, in that they at least waited until a corpse washed on shore before severing the finger!

Even if the wreckers of Long Beach Island are pure conjecture, and if their horrid methodology is mere legend, there is absolute proof that many early islanders did avail themselves of the leavings of a shipwreck. That proof is in the timbers of many buildings, the artifacts and "treasures" in many homes, and the memories of many an islander still alive today.

Indeed, one long-time Barnegat Light resident whose desires to remain anonymous we shall honor, tells of an incident that took place not too many years ago near the northern tip of Long Beach.

It seems that a cargo of castor beans spilled from a freighter offshore. The crates washed onto the beach and, in the true spirit of "finders keepers . . ." and whatnot, the finders did keep. These finders, however, decided to try a

4

dastardly practical joke on the crew of the local Coast Guard installation.

Telling the seamen that the beans were an exotic, tasty delicacy, they urged them to "enjoy!" The castor beans were not the tastiest thing the men ever ate, but in the spirit of fellowship with the "townies," they accommodated them. You can probably guess the rest. The result crippled the Coast Guard Station for weeks!

There are other assorted and varied accounts of islanders' use of wit and wisdom regarding pilfered or found cargo. So precious to sailors was liquor many years ago, that they would trade just about anything for a bottle. Such was the deal struck between an islander with a bottle of hooch and a mate with a cargo of coffee. The trade for the bottle kept Barnegat Light residents in coffee for an entire long, cold winter!

Through the years, many islanders have fought valiantly to discredit the legends of "wreckers," "pirates," and the like. Toward this effort, nearly every shard of information and bit of research stops short of confirming any cruel and inhumane activity by any Long Beach Islander, then or now. In 1835, a Philadelphia newspaper published a lurid account of alleged piracy at Barnegat. The victims of a packet ship wreck claimed they were robbed by "miscreants" waiting in the surf. The next week, the same paper printed an apology, noting that the robberies were more likely committed by the sailors of the ship.

Still, those who spread the rumors of piracy were able to walk that fine line of definition of the word "pirate." They also had several bona fide cases upon which to base their tales. As far back as the mid-eighteenth century, there was evidence that privateers used Barnegat Inlet as a safe haven to escape after their raids on British shipping. Later, there were documented cases of trials and convictions of those who looted ships stranded on the Barnegat Shoals.

So the legend of the "Barnegat Pirates" and the "wreckers" remains intact, and a stopping-off point for those whose thoughts ponder the past of Long Beach. The "mooncussers" of Cape Cod have been memorialized in song and verse. The "wreckers" of Cape Hatteras have even been remembered in the name of one of that cape's towns — the town named for the beasts that carried the lantern that lured the ships to the shoals — "Nag's Head."

Here on Long Beach Island, these notions are merely stories. But as Gustav Kobbe, in his 1889 book "The Jersey Coast and Pines," said so eloquently: "When one reflects upon the terror of a storm at sea; the joy with which the tempest-tossed mariner must have beheld what seemed to be familiar beacon; and the despair that must have come over him when he saw the line of hissing breakers ahead, and realized that he had been lured to certain death, one fails to find words strong enough to express one's sense of the villainy of the Pirates of Barnegat."

# THE SOBBING GHOST
# OF LONG BEACH ISLAND, N.J.

On a warm, summer day, the beaches of Beach Haven, Surf City and towns the length of Long Beach Island are sandy playgrounds that play host to volleyball, sunbathing, girl and boy watching, and swimming. There is laughter, music, and quiet relaxation.

By night, the beach can become a foreboding place. The sea breeze wafts through grassy dunes, playing mournful tricks on the ears. The relentless, eternal surf roars in and whispers out in a ceaseless cacophony which confuses the senses. Fogs and mists tantalize the eyes. A tangled clump of seaweed a hundred yards up the beach is a frightening, gruesome thing to approach with cautious care in case it is not what it is.

The beach at night is home only to the nocturnal creatures that feed on it, cavort on it, and die on it. To most of those people who revel in it under the sun, the beach by the dark of night is a fearsome experience.

It is said that on the darkest of evenings, when the moon is new or shrouded by thick clouds, the ghost of a young woman walks in eternal sorrow from one end of the island to the other. Her plaintive sighs are not unlike the whisper of the receding surf and the windswept songs of the dunes. But somehow, they are more recognizable as the pitiful pleas of a girl.

Legend has it that the maiden's heart was first to break, then her mind and spirit were shattered, and finally her lonely life was ended in utter misery. She never recovered from one incredible experience that touched off the tragic chain of events.

Her story harkens back to the tales of "wreckers" on Long Beach Island. She was an unwitting member of a band of these beach bandits, of which her father was the leader. Blindly obeying his wishes, she would follow his gang to the surf each time a ship met its fate on the shoals, or at the hand of the tempests.

One particular night, a storm brewed off shore. The lights of a brig were visible, bobbing violently in the distance. The lights seemed to get brighter, bigger. It was apparent that the ship would soon succumb to the storm and become another victim of the unpredictable and unbridled ocean.

The wreckers assembled on the beach, ready to pillage the hulk. Sure enough, the screams of twisting timbers and hopeless people could be discerned above the roar of the surf. The helpless ship, in its dying gasps, floated closer and closer to the shore.

Soon, bits of flotsam appeared in the waves. Then, bodies. Miserable corpses, some with their faces contorted in their dying anguish, rolled onto the sand as unceremoniously as the wrack and tangle of seaweed.

The task of these people was morbidly simple. As the dead reached the land, their bodies would be stripped of any worthwhile adornments.

The grisly thievery was proceeding well until a ghastly scream split the night. Members of the party looked toward the young woman, whose arms were flailing about as she knelt beside one of the bodies.

The girl's father, confused by her actions, whisked her away to higher ground. He calmed her down and urged her to explain her sudden display of grief.

Through uncontrollable sobs, she tried to tell her story. The words did not come. She grasped her father's hand and ran with him to the cadaver that sparked her outburst. It was face down in the wet sand. The man was instructed, through now-crazed and incoherent yelps, to roll the victim onto his back. The father took a shoulder and did so. As the face became visible, a shudder of pity, fear and outrage shot through the man's being. The body was that of his daughter's lover.

He had joined the crew of the ship being ravished by the wreckers, and fate brought him and his lady friend back together in one final, cruel moment.

It is believed the young woman suffered much following the incident. Her heart and mind broken, she weakened and died in short order.

Today, her ghost walks the beaches from Barnegat Light to Beach Haven, in a never-ending search for redemption. Beware, should you walk the shoreline on a moonless night. That shadowy figure just beyond your clear vision could be her spectral form. The melancholy moaning you think is the breeze could be her perpetual weeping.

Beware!

# THE BRANT BEACH GHOST

One need not set a supernatural stage when speaking with Surf City resident Alyce Crowe. She has seen the dramas of ghosts and monsters play out before her many times.

A charming writer, psychic and keeper of Long Beach legends, Alyce believes in the charms, and yes, the mysteries of this island. She believes because she has experienced, first hand, a bit of both.

She speaks of a small house just off Long Beach Boulevard on 11th Street in Surf City, where the senses of those with psychic awareness are tempted by an unknown presence. "There are not 'ghost stories' connected to it," she ponders, "but if you are sensitive at all, you will feel it. Every time I bicycle past it, it spooks me."

Alyce doesn't see ghosts behind every sand dune, or mysteries in every darkened side street. But her family's experiences, and indeed her own encounters with the surreal world have made her quite aware that the unseen, the unknown, is quite real.

There is the story of strange happenings in the Union Church, at 19th and the Boulevard in Surf City. It is within the sanctuary walls that, if eyewitness accounts are to be believed, the spirit of its former minister, Albert Elijah Morris, is still very evident.

This spirit has been felt, and especially HEARD on several occasions, by more than one person. As members of the congregation went about their business days, weeks and months after Rev. Morris' death, they could hear his distinctive voice bellowing from within the church. By name, the voice called to these unsuspecting folks who, in the end, were not so much terrified but comforted somehow by its presence.

Alyce Crowe's tales run the ghostly gamut from this ethereal example to the story of a sea serpent off Surf City and a ghost in a house in Brant Beach.

Virtually all seacoast settlements have some sort of "sea serpent" or "sea monster" narratives within the ledgers of their legends.

One longtime resident of Holgate's recounts the story of a strange sighting he and another (now deceased) man once made just off the coast of the village on the island's southern tip.

"We were heading out of the bay one sunshiny day," the bearded, bedraggled fisherman says, "and all was well. The blues were running, so we were headed out to get our share. We were rounding the end of the island when we saw this very strange, uh, this thing in the water.

"We had a pair of binoculars aboard, so I went in the cabin for them. It was no use, though. The lenses were all salted, and the boat was hitting the waves too hard to hold them steady anyway.

"I said to my buddy, 'do you see what I see?' He mumbled something, nodded his head yes, and never blinked away from looking at it. It wasn't a whale, or a porpoise. It didn't jump out of the water, it looked a little like a belly-up boat, which I think we both figured it was for the longest time.

"We steered over closer to it and the sunshine sort of reflected off it. It was no overturned boat. It had big scales, maybe two or three inches square. It had what looked to be very large gills or openings in its side. There were no fins, but a very large eye on the side toward us.

"The thing just rested dead in the water as we got closer. Then, all of a sudden, it turned really quick, sort of pivoting around.

It looked squarely at us and lifted its head. It's mouth opened real wide, and there were big, pointed teeth. It looked like we disturbed it. It came back down with a splash and sank under the water."

The old man's voice quivered as he told his story. His speech was punctuated with sighs and head shaking indicating disbelief. Still, he swore that every word was true, and to this day, neither of the men could explain what they were witnessing.

Alyce Crowe may have provided an answer.

"Others have seen it, or something like it, she says, referring to a Long Beach Island sea monster often referred to by a man she identifies only as "Uncle Rube."

"I've heard his last name spelled 'Corliss,' or 'Corleis,' and whatever. But this Uncle Rube swore up and down that he'd seen a sea serpent out there, mostly off the Surf City beaches."

Like the man who related the above story, this "Uncle Rube" was quite familiar with the animals that populate the bay and ocean. Not prone to conjure up mythical monsters, these men stand by their stories and give not a damn if they are not believed. Just as well-respected pilots and even astronauts see "unidentified flying objects" in the course of their lengthy airborne careers, so too do mariners witness strange swimming creatures. Some of these unidentified creatures swim the waters around Long Beach Island.

Returning to land, however, we are intrigued by another "ghost story" from the memory of Alyce Crowe. Again, she stands by the account, especially considering her connection with it.

"My relatives had a home on 42nd Street in Brant Beach, up on Ocean Drive," she says. "My grandmother, and everyone else, loved the place.

"My grandfather passed away, but grandmother continued to live there, all of us knowing how fond she was of the house. She seemed to take her husband's death well, and we all thought that she would stay there and be happy.

"Shortly after the funeral, though, my stepmother found out that grandmother intended to sell the house. We were all

12

shocked. My stepmother was downright heartbroken. She wondered why.

"Now, my grandmother was not one to see things. She was a fine woman, and very sensible. Finally, though, she revealed to all why she wanted to leave this home. Quite simply put, it was haunted!"

The haunting took the form of her deceased husband. His mortal remains buried, his spirit continued to walk the floors of the house that was so dear to him in life.

His ghost was present always. And always, the same sad routine was repeated. The ghostly figure appeared in the bedroom, sat on the side of the bed and put on its shoes. There was no conversation, no attempt to communicate, just the seemingly-detached spectre manifesting itself in this melancholy ritual.

"It got the best of grandmother," Alyce relates. "She told us she had to leave because of this, this ghost. It's a prime example of a good piece of property let go because of fear."

Alyce Crowe finds fascination in these strange stories that run through the fibre of life on Long Beach. That fibre, she believes, is many-colored and reinforced by the kind of person who calls the island their home.

"The people of this island are very incurious," she states firmly, and with conviction. "Here, on Long Beach Island, you can be exactly what you want to be, and do exactly what you want to do. This is the island of second chance."

Yes, Alyce, and perhaps even the spirits of these people find a "second chance," as well.

# THE BEACH HAVEN STABBER
# AND OTHER STORIES

Call it a legend, call it a tall tale, or call it a simple story designed to scare the daylights out of children who have been naughty.

For at least one longtime Surf City resident and prominent businessman, however, the story of the "Beach Haven Stabber" is indelibly imprinted in his memory.

The exact names and addresses are not important. Even in the following text, generalizations may come too dangerously close to reality.

The story begins with the purchase of an old house in Beach Haven, a house that once belonged to a physician. The fine home featured all the amenities of a shore home, but went one or two steps beyond the norm.

The house had built into it a wine cellar, with a dirt floor. It was a dark, dank place, and added character to the dwelling. Also evident in the floor plan was a makeshift operating room downstairs, complete with leftover instruments and equipment.

Being one of a handful of doctors' offices on the island, it was the scene of many exciting and crucial events. One event, however, sparked the "stabber" legend and brought goosebumps to the flesh of all who would know the house from then on.

There was an unfortunate incident on the streets of Beach Haven one night. A fight erupted. A man was stabbed. He needed help.

The victim was taken to the closest doctor's office for treatment, pending further care at the hospital on the mainland. By the time the stabbing victim reached the Beach Haven M.D.'s examining table it was too late. He died in the house.

A search for the killer turned up nothing.

It is said that still today, the ghost of this unfortunate man waits inside the Beach Haven house. Confused, and seeking vengeance for his untimely death, he lingers through eternity.

Young children living in, and nearby the house knew of the haunting. Even the older folks suspected there may be something to the story. They threatened to send the children to what was the operating room if they didn't behave. They told the children the ghost would rise and take out its fury on them. The restless wraith would materialize, ghostly blood would drip from the stab wound, and . . . and . . .

The children were well behaved most of the time!


From the same storyteller comes another saga, set in a beach-front house on the south end of Beach Haven.

The people who owned the idyllic home had a large dog which loved to romp in the sand. They'd tie the dog out on the beach on summer evenings, and most of the time the contented pet would frolic with the sand crabs, dig incessantly, and playfully bother any occasional beachcombers.

One night, the dog started to bark. At first, it was nothing out of the ordinary to the dog's owners. Soon enough, though, the barking became furious and incessant. They ventured to a beachside window to see what had disturbed the dog.

The dog's attention was riveted toward the sea. As if affixed toward an invisible being, the dog strained its leash and bayed into the darkness.

The man of the house shouted at the dog. Yelling to it to be quiet, the spell was finally broken and the dog glanced toward the house. There was a strange look in its eyes, but it stopped barking.

No sooner did the family settle back into the house, the dog began its enraptured barking. They reasoned that something known only to the dog itself was intruding on its solace, and decided to wait a few minutes until reprimanding it again.

Within those few minutes, the barking stopped.

Figuring the distraction had gone away, the people relaxed. Surely, the dog would soon settle in and go to sleep, as it usually did, on the beach, near the porch.

Still, to make sure the dog was safe, the man went out to check just before heading for bed. To his horror, the dog was gone!

Beyond that fact, the dog's leash was still there, although crudely severed and ripped apart. Only a superhuman force could have torn the plastic-coated steel cord in that fashion, he thought.

Most frightening and puzzling of all, however, was a grotesque trail of blood and torn flesh leading from the dog's usual den to the ocean water. Paralleling this trail of blood were footprints — webbed footprints — leading out of the water, up to the severed leash, and back into the ocean!


Our storyteller, who operates one of the most visible and best-known businesses in Surf City, has more. His father swears he once saw a red-roofed, white-building village propped on the horizon a short distance from Holgate. Out fishing, he looked to the east, out to sea, and unmistakably saw the buildings — terra cotta roofs, almost Spanish in style. He knows well it couldn't have really been there. He blinked and rubbed his eyes, but it wouldn't go away.

Another very simple, but scary story is told by a Long Beach couple who witnessed it firsthand. They realize, too, that what happened couldn't have., but they know what they saw.

What they saw was a woman, walking down the Surf City beach a few yards behind them. This figure caught their eyes because it was dressed in very dated clothing, and strolling aimlessly as if in search of someone or something.

Nervously, the couple glanced over their shoulders from time to time to track the wanderings of the mysterious woman. They looked as she made a deliberate, jerking turn to the right, and walked slowly and deliberately . . . into the ocean.

She never emerged.

# THE NAMING OF SHIP BOTTOM

Most of the town names on Long Beach Island are easily traced. The island's position against the sea has yielded "Beach Haven," "Surf City" and "Spray Beach."

Barnegat Light is a tribute to the lighthouse, with "Barnegat" presumably originating in the Dutch word for "breakers." Holgate and Loveladies are the names of individuals who settled those areas.

But "Ship Bottom?"

Why would anyone give this enigmatic name to a town?

The answer to that question provides yet another "Legend of Long Beach Island."

Actually, there is some dispute about the relevant facts concerning the name. Of two versions of the event that led to the monicker, both are similar in context, but different in detail.

Version one places the year at 1817. The savage sea reared its ugly head as a storm twisted its way along the coast. It was not a fit day for ships coasting up or down the shipping lanes. To venture far from land was to court danger. To venture too closely to the shore was to tempt the shoals of Barnegat and the strong currents that could drag even the sturdiest three-master into perilously shallow waters.

There were few residents of the island at that time, but one apparently was the sea captain, Stephen Willets. Aware that the storm was endangering any craft unfortunate enough to be caught in its maelstrom, Captain Willets kept a sharp eye

18

through a spyglass for any glimpse of lights or silhouettes of ships in distress.

He ventured onto the beach as the storm subsided, to check any damage done and hoped against hope that no tell-tale signs of shipwrecks would be found. All hope was shattered when he saw, faintly in the distance, a large vessel, bottom up in the surf.

Captain Willets broke from a walk to a jog as he set his sights upon the beached ship. He arrived at its hulk, only to discover that there were no signs of life. The decks were hopelessly strewn with wreckage, and the surf was littered with corpses.

He surveyed the tragic scene, reckoning with the probability that all had been drowned in the wreck.

The howl of the wind was subsiding, but the relentless roar pounded in his ears. Somehow, there was another sound filtering through this rumbling.

Faintly, ever so faintly, he heard it. "Rap . . . rap . . . rap," it went, as if coming from the angry sea itself.

"Thump . . . thump . . .," it continued. Captain Willets cocked an ear toward the hull of the ship. "Good God," he thought, "the rapping sound is coming from within the ship!" His thoughts turned to words, and although there was no one nearby to receive them, he gasped, "Someone is in there. They're alive!"

Unbeknownst to the captain, there actually were people near him to hear his utterance. From the dunes they descended, ready to lend their hands in the rescue.

A rescue it would be. Although the wreck brought death to the others, it became obvious as the rapping sound from inside the hull intensified that someone had survived.

Using crude tools to chop through the massive timbers of the ship, the rescue party focused its attention at the source of the knocking sound. They chopped and chopped and after agonizing minutes broke through.

One of the men lifted a lantern to the small hole. Inside were dark eyes staring back at them. The desperate rapping turned into sobs of both joy and sorrow. The sole survivor of the wreck was about to be freed.

They continued to cut through the planking, until a fair-sized opening was made. Captain Willets reached inside, offering his hand in relief. Timidly, the survivor clasped his arm, and crawled cautiously through the hole.

It was a young woman.

She was, even in her bedraggled condition, possessed of an exotic beauty. Her terrible experience behind her, and now safe in the company of rescuers, she wept and uttered strange words of thanks.

While no one understood her, they did realize that she was grateful for their efforts, and her salvation.

There was a higher authority to be thanked, however. Still hysterically babbling in whatever language she employed, she dropped to her knees and drew a cross on the sand. All knew through this universal symbol that she was showing gratitude.

It's not known what happened to the beautiful foreigner from that point. Some say she was taken to New York City to begin her new life. Others say she remained on Long Beach Island and may even have married one of her rescuers.

In any event, the legend of her rescue remained long after it took place. As houses and hotels developed around the area, folks spoke of the time the men rescued the young woman from the bottom of the ship — the "Ship Bottom!"

# LITTLE MISS AUGUST
# ... THE YOUNG GHOST OF BEACH HAVEN

The dunes of any shoreline after dark lend themselves to the propagation of tales of mystery and intrigue. So too, do the swamps and meadows that form in the tidal waters that separate the island from the mainland.

There is much of the stuff of legends that abounds on Long Beach Island, but this story lacks much of it.

It is told by five members of a family, all of whom have visited Beach Haven for more than a dozen summers. They are solid citizens of Cherry Hill, New Jersey, both husband and wife in the professions and each child now at prestigious colleges in Pennsylvania.

Because they fear the ridicule and suspicion that surrounds the telling of "ghost stories," they ask that their names be changed in return for their story. Accommodating them, we trust their anonymity will not taint their credibility.

Let us call them Doug and Diane, and their children Kathy, Bess and Todd.

It is noted that their story lacks many of the elements of the classic ghost story because it played out on a crowded beach, in a lively restaurant, and in a comfortable beach home. It involved not a willowy figure in the fog, or a pirate's curse, but a very real and very young girl.

Young, for certain. Real? You decide.

The family shared a beach house in Beach Haven with a group of friends in Cherry Hill. Lucky for all, some members of the partnership preferred to occupy the place on the "off season," allowing fair access to all when they wanted.

The month of August belonged to this particular family, however, and every year, they would (and still do) spend the entire month at the oceanside retreat. Doug tried his hand at painting, Diane used the weeks as a relaxing escape from her rigorous job, and the kids burned off the energy of late summer and did what kids do "down the shore."

In August, 1982, the family moved into the house, quickly and methodically arranging it to suit their needs for the next four weeks or so. The bedrooms were promptly arranged with the family's belongings, and their lives shifted gears from the rush of the suburbs to the release of Long Beach Island.

As had been the tradition for perhaps a half-dozen years, Doug quickly set up his easel, canvas and palette, and was anxious to begin his painting.

He was a fair to good artist. His summertime masterpieces adorned his Cherry Hill home, his office, his wife's office, and the homes of close friends who were beneficiaries of his efforts at Christmas.

Throughout the year, Doug saved photographs from magazines, figuring he'd re-create them on canvas in August. This year, he thought he'd try something different. All along, a most lovely subject for a painting had eluded him, although it was ever-present and all around him. He decided this year to paint a seascape.

Granted, the view from the house lacked the rocky coastline, the lighthouse, and much of the romance of the average seascape. Still, there was a rickety snowfence undulating through the dunes, with sharp blades of dune grass spiking into the view. It was simply stated, but effective enough for an interesting piece.

The second day at the beach house, the first brush strokes were applied to the canvas. By the end of the first week, the painting was well along. Doug was pleased with its progress, and Diane — his harshest critic — agreed that it would be a fine addition to their personal collection of Doug's efforts.

After a busy day of activities on the beach during the second week of their stay, Doug retired to his studio to put the finishing touches on the painting. He had already decided on a title for it, "August." A bit vague, perhaps, but all in the family would know its significance.

Weary from the play and the work of a typical day of beach home ownership, Doug and Diane trod the spiraling staircase to their bedroom. It would be unusually quiet that night, with the children away at sleepovers at friends' homes.

All that follows may be disconcerting, and even implausible, but both Doug and Diane swear that it is, every word, true.

There are several signs an interviewer can detect that add credibility to an otherwise incredible story. All of those signs were evident in Doug and Diane's testimony as we sat in their home, a notepad filling rapidly with their tale.

Doug's lips quivered, and he swallowed firmly as if to gather strength for the story he was about to tell. Diane clasped her husband's hand in support, ready to add her words of endorsement.

"You've got to understand up front," Doug began, "that Diane and I do not go around seeing things. Fact is, we're both maybe a little too rational and realistic about things. I guess you might say we're sort of dull and stoic about life. We certainly don't, as they say, 'believe in ghosts.' "

Diane nodded in accordance with Doug's assessment of their approach to the supernatural, but added, "Maybe what happened to us that week has some sort of explanation, but neither of us can figure out how."

The night in question started out quietly, Doug and Diane both in their bed, both nearly exhausted from the day's activities. "I must admit that the painting was on my mind," Doug said, "I was sort of proud of it, but realized that it needed something — I didn't know what, but something. I won't attempt to compare it at all, but it was something like the Mona Lisa. Without that something, that crooked smile, chances are it would just have gone down into history as another portrait of some woman. Da Vinci added that extra 'something' and it all worked for him. As I say, don't think I'm comparing my little painting with the Mona Lisa, but I think you know what I mean.

"Anyway, I guess we both fell asleep rather quickly that night, and it was so very, very quiet. The kids were older now, and able to fend for themselves. It was one of the first times Diane and I had the place to ourselves.

"Of course, I don't really remember falling asleep. But I do remember what happened sometime during the night. It was the weirdest, most frightening thing that ever happened to me."

So vivid in Doug's memory is the event of the night that he stumbles for words. Lighting a cigarette and reaching for another swig of his soft drink, he bolsters himself for the next chapter.

"Well, I was asleep. I must have been, because I know we went upstairs at about 11:30 that night, and I woke up in pitch darkness and saw 3:13 on the clock. It's the first thing I saw when I awakened.

"I was really confused. I sat up, looked again at the clock and wondered why I was awake. I started to look around the room when I saw her. A little girl. She was maybe four or five feet away from me, standing at the side of the bed. She scared me half to death. I might have still been half asleep up to that point, but you'd better believe that I was fully awake when I looked over and saw her!"

The words come more slowly from Doug's lips, now, and despite the near-chilling air conditioner, there are beads of sweat forming on his forehead.

"I tried to figure out in a split-second what was happening, who she was, how she got into the house, why she was there, and at the same time I debated whether or not to wake up Diane. It was as confusing as it was frightening.

"I guess I settled down a bit, and kept looking at her. She really didn't seem to see me. The light of the digital clock, a

24

kind of greenish glow, was all that illuminated her. That, of course, added to the eeriness of it all.

"She looked toward me, but seemed to be looking a foot or two over me. I didn't know what to say, but I think I whispered something really stupid like, 'can I help you?' or something like that.

"I know one thing that made me realize that I was awake. I quickly gathered up the sheets and covered myself. I sleep in the nude, you know, and here was this little girl a couple of feet away! What a time for modesty!

"As I started to get my senses about me, I said something again. I asked her if she was lost, or in trouble. She just kept staring over my head. I thought of turning on a light, but the closest one was on the night stand on Diane's side of the bed, and I didn't want to disturb her yet. It turned out, though, that I wouldn't need a light. That's one of the scariest things about the whole thing.

"The little girl stood very rigid, not moving at all. She didn't respond to my questions, and I began to think I was imagining the whole thing. Then, as I tried to figure out what to do next, she slowly, but almost mechanically, raised her left hand. She pointed it straight out, again just a foot or so above my head. It was only then that I realized something. She was soaking wet.

Water dripped from her sleeve as she lifted her arm.

"Then, there was whimpering. She began to whimper, almost like a small dog would. Now, I was very terrified. It all seemed like something out of a cheap horror movie or the "Twilight Zone" or something. But it was really happening, and happening to me."

At this point, Doug says he was very aware of his surroundings, and knew that he was not dreaming or imagining the vision of the little girl. He took notice of her dress. "She was wearing a long dress, and it looked like it was torn in many places. She was facing me, but it looked as if the whole back part of the dress might have been torn off.

"She just stood there, whimpering and sometimes making a gurgling sound. I settled down a little, and felt that she needed help. It was awkward, though. There was very little light, just the glow from the streetlight outside and a night light in the bedroom, as well as the clock's light."

Describing the girl, Doug said she appeared to be quite pretty, perhaps ten years old, and possessing long hair that was matted and soaked.

"In one burst of courage," Doug continued, "I stood up, and gently pulled the sheet from the bed so as not to disturb Diane. I wrapped it around myself and decided to go help the girl. By now, I figured that Diane might as well wake up and find out what was going on.

"I kept my eyes on the girl as I walked around the front of the bed, going over to Diane's side to turn on a light. As I did this, she began to walk backwards toward the sliding glass doors that go out to the beachside porch. I quickened my pace and whispered for her to stay. I really wanted to help her now. By the time I reached the light switch, she was near the glass doors. I turned on the light, jostled Diane awake, and in that split-second that I looked away, she was gone. She just, well, she just disappeared onto the porch.

"Diane was stirring, and I was trying to deal with her at the same time I was trying to figure out what had happened to the little visitor. Then it struck me, like a ton of bricks, that she really did just disappear. What's more, she backed out — I saw her back out of the window, right through the window. There's no doubt in my mind that she simply walked through the full-length glass doors, onto the back porch."

Diane verified the events that now started to involve her.

"I remember Doug pushing on my shoulder," she relates, "and flicking on the light. I had no idea why he was doing this, and at first was a little disturbed about it. Then, it hit me that maybe something had happened to one of the children. I woke up right away, fearing the worst.

"About all I really remember then is Doug, with the sheet tied around him like a toga, whispering some words toward the beach porch. I looked over toward the sliding glass doors and saw something, a shadow or something, but I honestly can't tell you I saw any little girl."

Diane's and Doug's stories dovetail at this point, when both became involved in the mystery.

"I turned the light on, knew Diane was awake, and was trying to explain to myself what had happened," Doug recalls. "The little girl, or whatever, was gone, and I really didn't look forward to explaining to Diane why I was up and so very frightened. I knew that she'd think I was just dreaming, but I also knew that I absolutely was not!

"Diane did ask right away if I was all right, and if the kids were all right. I assured her yes on both counts. Then, she asked if I just had a nightmare. I told her no, and got a little angry, or maybe hurt, when she started to smile a little. I know that what I was telling her sounded unbelievable, but I didn't need any ridicule at that point.

"Diane got up, slipped on a nightie, and sat on the end of the bed as I told her more. Then it hit me — if that little girl was really soaking wet, there'd be a puddle, or at least a wet floor, where she stood. I grabbed Diane's hand and went around the bed to where the girl was standing. I was shocked, and confused when there was no evidence whatsoever of any wetness. Diane seemed to be a bit more understanding, and I hoped she realized that I was very scared. We retraced the movements of the little girl, to the glass doors and all. For some reason, we opened the doors and went out on the porch as I continued to tell her my story. Then, a most unbelievable thing happened. I looked down on the porch and saw what seemed to be a very small piece of torn cloth. It was wet and gray, and looked very old. There were no footsteps or anything, just this piece of cloth — about the size of a cigar. I reached down, picked it up and it crumbled in my hand. There's no doubt that it was cloth, even Diane recognized that. But it was very brittle and just disintegrated as I lifted it."

Diane added that the cloth, a strip about an inch wide and four or five inches long, did appear to be crinoline, and something of which a little girl's dress would be made.

Diane took up the story from there. "When I saw that piece of cloth, I got chills. I guess I really did believe Doug all along. As he said, he's not one to see things, and never really had any nightmares or weird dreams. But you know, it's tough trying to understand something like this.

"I remember that we were holding hands and I think Doug was close to tears as he tried to calm down. Suddenly, I happened to look down over the dune to the beach when I saw it. There, silhouetted in the little bit of moonlight there, was a little girl. She was walking slowly on the beach, sort of diagonally toward the water. From Doug's description of her dress, I felt this had to be her.

"My motherly instincts then prevailed, and I thought that I'd better help her. It was, what, four in the morning, and this little girl was wandering on the beach? It was very strange.

"Doug and I both saw the figure. He was still a little bit put out by everything, and it took a few moments for me to convince him to come along to the beach with me to see what was wrong with the little girl. Then, Doug hit me squarely with a word I never heard him use before. He told me he wasn't about to go the girl, because it was a 'ghost.'

"Really, we are so realistic about life and, I guess, square, that ghosts and goblins and all that to us are just things kids dress up as at Halloween. It really shocked me when Doug referred to this girl as a ghost. I knew that he was very, very scared." In the minute or two of discussion between Doug and Diane, something very bizarre had happened. They both looked again toward the little girl and watched with utter amazement as she slowly walked into the surf, deeper and deeper into the water, seemingly unaffected by the rushing waves, and disappeared.

"We both just stood there wide-eyed," Doug said. "I felt my knees starting to buckle and I don't think I blinked my eyes or breathed for about two or three minutes. Obviously, I had never seen anything like this in my life.

"For a few seconds, I thought that I'd better call the police. Maybe this was all very real, and this little girl was really in trouble. I thought again, though, and felt that it might have been very real, but the girl was not real at all. I told myself, against all logic and personal beliefs, that I — and now Diane — just witnessed the presence of a ghost."

Doug paused, lit another cigarette, and slumped in his chair. His story was told, his pragmatism was shattered, and his conscience was bared.

But the story was not, by any stretch of the imagination, complete. There was much more to be told, and what was to follow would test even the strongest constitution. Doug continued his story.

"Somehow, Diane and I managed to calm down enough to go back to bed. I looked over at the clock and saw that it was 3:41 in the morning. It seemed that the episode took so much longer, but it all happened rather quickly. I think that we were both too shaken by the experience to go back to sleep quickly, but I remember dozing off until the sun was up the next morning.

It was just after 9 o'clock when I heard some stirring downstairs. I heard Bess and Kathy's voices and realized that they were coming home from their overnight party down the street.

Diane was already up and getting dressed, and we would soon go down for some breakfast. Diane and I looked at each other, both knowing what we were thinking. Should we tell the children what we went through last night, or just keep quiet about it? As it turned out, we had no choice.

"Kathy and Bess started up the stairs to their room, which is next to ours, when I heard Bess say something about my painting. It was on the easel downstairs, and as you came in the front door, you could see it. Anyway, Bess said something like, "I sure like what dad did to the painting. That makes it complete.'

"The girls got upstairs, and I asked them what Bess just said. She was real bubbly, and told me she liked the little addition I made to the painting, that it gave it that little extra that made it stand out. I hadn't worked on the piece since the last time the girls saw it, and I wondered what she was talking about.

She told me 'the little girl.' That little girl I added to the painting, she said, was what it needed!"

Later, Bess confirmed that the conversation took place, and added that she thought at the time that her father looked somewhat drained and confused.

Doug continued, "I rushed down the stairs to the corner of the living room I use as a studio and damned if it wasn't there. Standing on the beach of my scene was a little girl, her back toward the point-of-view, staring out to sea. She was wet, and her dress was torn up the back.

"I swear to you that I never touched that painting since the previous afternoon. Don't ask me how that little girl was added to it, because I don't know. I looked at it for a long time, said nothing to the girls or Diane, but I know that Diane knew exactly what I was feeling."

Doug said he felt ill at that point, and dropped onto the sofa to sort things out. "I really thought I was going crazy," he said. "Or maybe it was an elaborate joke. I knew better, though. There was no way to explain any of it now."

Diane took the girls aside and related the incidents of the night. All were now very frightened, and dazed by the inexplicable chain of events.

The story is still not over, and it may never end.

Diane added yet another element to the mystery: "The whole thing just kept getting more and more unbelievable. As if all we went through wasn't enough, a couple of days — or maybe a week — later, somebody broke into our house in Beach Haven. We were all together, at a friend's house, until about midnight one night. When we got back to our place, we noticed that the door from the bottom floor was open. The whole door knob was broken apart. Right away, we all thought the worst.

"We immediately went to a neighbor's house and called the police.

We stayed there, keeping watch on our house just in case whoever broke in might still be inside. The police officer got there in a few minutes, and checked. He called us in, to check on what was taken.

"Of course, the television, stereo, and a couple of small appliances were gone. There wasn't any real damage done, but all together, the thieves got away with a couple of thousand dollars worth of things. Then it hit me. I looked over and saw that Doug's seascape was missing. The easel was bare."

Doug adds to the story, "That was really strange. First, if any thief tried to sell that painting, he'd have a hard time. I'm no Rembrandt. But even if he managed to do so, it seems to me that it could be traced very easily. Suppose by some chance that one of us saw it somewhere after it had been fenced. It seems that it would be very risky for any thief to try and get away with anything so dumb."

Other original works of art were taken from the walls of the house. "This guy, or guys, must have had a van or something," Doug laments. "Some of those paintings were really large. All of them had a lot of sentimental attachment, too."

The burglary was never solved, and the paintings have not yet been found.

There remains one more chapter in this far-reaching and perhaps far-fetched saga, and one more family member who tells it.

Doug and Diane's son, Todd, was detached somewhat from the summer's mysteries. "He's hardly ever around," Diane said. "One day, though, he became a part of all this strange stuff."

"Mom and dad told me about what happened to them," Todd said. "I have to believe them. They really are straight people — too straight, sometimes. When Bess and I once kidded with them about their 'ghost,' and went "whooooo," they really got mad. They would never, ever, make something like this up just to get attention.

"Like mom said, I'm never really around much. I've got a job up in Manahawkin at night, and I sleep in the mornings. Even then, I'm usually at a friend's house. In the afternoons, I'm either there or on the beach.

"It's easy to remember when what happened to me took place because it was the last day we were down here in 1982. I had the previous night off, so I had the whole day to myself.

"I picked up my friend, and we decided we'd celebrate the end of the summer with a big meal at the best place in town and a final fling on the beach. It wasn't like in some rock and roll song, where we part tearfully, because we go to the same university, and we'll see each other there the next week.

"Well, we went to a real good restaurant — I guess I shouldn't mention it by name — and sat down for our big meal. We got a window seat overlooking the sidewalk. Very nonchalantly, I pulled back the curtains to look outside. I almost shit!

"Like a flashback, everything mom and dad told me about their experience hit me. I was really stunned for a second. Standing right outside our window was a little girl, looking just like the one in mom and dad's story. She was about ten, soaking wet, matted hair, and her dress was in shreds in the back. She just stood there, her back to me, looking into the street.

"Now, you're not going to believe this, but when I told my friend to look outside — in that little bit of time that took — she was gone. It was broad daylight, on a busy street, but she was gone. I had never told my friend about my parents' experience, so I just clammed up and said I saw someone we knew pass by. I kept the secret, but I was churning inside with a little fear and a lot of confusion."

Later that day, Todd and his friend went for their "last fling" on the beach. It was, as well, the "last fling" of the mysterious girl in tattered clothing.

"We just settled onto the beach," Todd remembers, "and laid down on the blanket to catch some sun. It wasn't a typical hot, August day, but it was fairly warm. The beach wasn't really crowded, and hardly anybody was really in the water.

"I remember that I was kneeling on all fours, facing the dunes, trying to zero in on a radio station. Once again, I couldn't believe my eyes.

"I was distracted by movement right on the edge of the beach. I looked up, squinted to see whatever it was, and then like something out of a cheap movie, she was there. It was that damned little girl again. And again, her back was toward me.

She had the same torn dress, was soaking wet, and just stood there in the sand. I tried to keep my eye on her as long as possible and get my friend's attention, but it was no use. I must have blinked or something, and the figure was gone. It was the absolute strangest and scariest thing that's ever happened to me," Todd concludes.

Doug has since tried to find any connection between his beach house and any possibility of a ghost. He has found nothing. He's never told the story to any of the co-owners of the property, and feels a bit guilty about that. "I don't know, I guess I should," he said. "I've told them, of course, about the break-in, and we've taken precautions against that happening again. But I'm not sure I want to tell them about our experiences with the little girl, or whatever the hell she is or was."

Diane said the family came back the following August, with a certain amount of cautious hesitation. Nothing happened.

"Since then," Diane said, "we've learned to live with whatever happened to us. We even gave that little girl a name, 'Little Miss August.' It's really sad, though. What if she, or it, really is a ghost? What if it's the spirit of a shipwreck victim or something like that? Maybe it's trapped here on earth, at this place, and doesn't know who to turn to. I don't know, maybe the ghost painted herself into the painting in some desperate move for identity or something. I know it sounds, and probably is, impossible. I've done a lot of reading about apparitions, spirits, and things like that. Never did before, but have since I experienced it first hand. After reading about how the energy of the spirit or the soul can remain earthbound in a confused state, well, I kind of pity 'Little Miss August,' and wish I could help her. Who knows, maybe she'll come back some day."

# THE HADDOCK HOUSE
# AND ITS GHOSTLY WIDOW'S WALK

Perhaps the most mysterious and appealing architectural appointments to the classic "shore homes" of Long Beach Island is the "Widow's Walk."

Sometimes enclosed, sometimes not, these platforms in the middle of the roofs were given their somber sobriquets because all too often, in the glorious days of sail, the person walking on them turned out to be a widow.

The "walk" served as a lookout perch for those seeking a good view of the sea. A standard fixture in the cramped compartment was a spyglass. From this vantage point, ships traversing the shipping lanes could be spotted, and eager wives waiting for their men to come home from the sea would be reassured when their ships were spied on the horizon.

It was those women whose husbands never returned who gave the name to the rooftop superstructure. For weeks, months and even years after their mariners' vessels were due back, they'd patiently but fruitlessly pace the floorboards; widows walking and hoping against all hope.

"From here, I have a marvelous view, maybe second only to the view from 'Old Barney' itself." The words belong to Richard Plunkett, a personable North Jersey native who speaks from atop the legendary Haddock House in Barnegat Light.

He is correct. Positioned squarely on the compass points, a glance north provides a sweeping view of the inlet.

34

East is the rising sun and the sea. South, Long Beach Island spreads out in all her glory. To the west, Barnegat Bay.

Plunkett's "Widow's Walk" is outfitted in the manner of his entire home. Elegant, functional, and saturated with the flavor of the sailing era, the house is a tribute to Plunkett's prowess as a professional antique dealer down the island.

He's lived there now for just over three years. His mind has resided there for decades. "My father was a professional baseball player for a Long Beach club," Plunkett says. "His team practiced at Beach Haven in the spring, and in the spring of my eighth year I saw this house for the first time. It was love at first sight. Every time in my life that I saw it, the love affair with it grew. Finally, I was able to buy it. It was like a dream come true."

What he bought was a home reeking with history and, mystery. It was once the home of John W. Haddock, whose name lives in the law journals of America, as the namesake of the "Haddock Rule," a legal precedent for certain kinds of divorce cases.

It is the word, "divorce" that triggered the chain of events that altered legal practice and the lives of Haddock, his family, and two women.

The details of the sticky legal battle are not terribly germane to the story you're about to read, but it is worth noting that Mr. Haddock, an inveterate womanizer, traveler and bon vivant, was of "old money," and after sowing his wild oats settled down with a young lady in the New York City area. The marriage failed, and Haddock divorced the woman in Connecticut. Soon after, he married another woman in New York. The first wife fought the second marriage, claiming the Connecticut divorce was not valid in New York. The ensuing legal maneuvering created quite a scandal, and resulted in Haddock's wealthy family virtually disowning him. Or, as the story goes.

This is not a soap opera, but a book on legends. Haddock himself has become somewhat of a legend in Barnegat Light, although few folks seem to know much about the man (and his women).

35

What is known is that Haddock was a benevolent man and a worthy collector of nautical artifacts. Haddock-owned nameplates, figureheads and other appurtenances can still be found in museums and private collections. Richard Plunkett has found evidence that Haddock provided for speaking tubes in his home, and hatch cover doors as well as numerous other items add a general nautical ambience to the place.

"The story goes that Haddock and his second wife saw the Barnegat Lighthouse from aboard a packet steamer going from Baltimore to New York," relates Plunkett. "They decided that that's where they wanted to live, so they bought some land near the lighthouse and built this house."

Actually, the house was originally located much farther north from its present site on Long Beach Island Boulevard. There is some dispute about when it was built (Plunkett says there is evidence that it was built circa 1885), but it is known that it was moved — lock, stock and haunted widow's walk — in 1915 after a savage storm ravaged the northern tip of Long Beach Island. The same storm destroyed more than a dozen homes, and remaining residents, including the proprietors of the famed Oceanic Hotel, decided to move farther inland.

Plunkett's tasteful additions to the Haddock House have served to enhance its atmosphere. "The place has its share of interesting quirks," he says. "On one wall, the word 'CON-TENT' is spelled out in brass studs, for whatever reason, and above the front door is the phrase, 'THE SUN NEVER SETS ON THIS DOOR' is still discernible."

There's just one problem with that last statement, however. The claim that the sun "never sets" on the front door might have been true in the home's original placement. At that time, the entrance might have faced east, north or south and indeed the sun never did set on the door. But when the building was moved, its main entrance and its bold statement was positioned on the streetside, facing west, where now the sun sets every evening on the front door.

Could this simple aberration be enough to lure John Haddock and his second wife to the house, both in eternal spirit form? Or is it the simple love for the home that keeps the couple there? Only their ghosts know for certain!

It is said that Haddock's second wife, Julia, so loved the views from the widow's walk that she'd spend endless hours there, leading a sheltered life, not exclusively because of the embarassment of the divorce case. The two were very close, but John's zest for life seemed to overpower Julia's equal zest for privacy.

John and Julia also so loved the lighthouse that towered over their lives that they vowed to be buried "in the beam of Barnegat." This desire was fulfilled, and today a handsome yet strikingly simple monument with one word, "HAD-DOCK," marks their graves on a slight knoll of a Waretown cemetery.

Do the ghosts of John and Julia Haddock walk the rooms, and especially the widow's walk of the home now owned by Richard Plunkett?

There is good evidence that the answer to that question is "yes."

Plunkett is very aware that he may not be alone even when he retires, by himself, in the Haddock House.

"There are definitely vibrations up there, especially on a full moon. It's very, uh, very . . ." Richard Plunkett's words trail off as he attempts to describe the presence, or presences, he's sensed on the widow's walk of his home. "I really don't believe in the spirit world, but sure enough whatever it is, it affects the whole house," he continues.

Indeed, there is an almost eerie feeling about the place. Its stormy history, and the tales of the island upon which it rests, seem to wrap around the visitor. Plunkett is not dismayed by the feeling. "It's not a bad presence," he says, "but there is definite energy up there."

Plunkett's attention is focused on the narrow staircase leading to the widow's walk. It is on the walk that it is said the ghosts of Mr. and Mrs. Haddock perambulate on nights of a full moon.

"I sleep up there in the summertime, and many times I

can feel the presence," says Plunkett. Sometimes I can hear what sounds like voices up there. There is a strange aura there, but I don't fear it — it's nothing bad."

Other friends, including a priest, have detected this aura. And if the theories of certain students of the paranormal are to be believed, perhaps Haddock's ghost has manifested itself in another creature of the realm. "Amid all the strange noises and sensations," Plunkett points out, "there is this one particular seagull. He's hung around here for years, always here, atop the chimney. He's sort of my 'guardian protector.' Just in case, I've named him 'Haddock!'

That morsel of levity aside, Plunkett does not treat the possibility that he dwells in a "haunted house" lightly. He has a great deal of respect for the life and times of John Haddock, and feels honored that his spirit may have chosen to remain earthbound and co-inhabit the house.

"In a way," Plunkett muses, "the presence is reassuring. I feel a kinship to Haddock, and I feel that his spirit approves of what I've done to his house."

# PIRATE TREASURE

Wherever the sand meets the sea, pirate legends are sure to abound. Why, then, should Long Beach Island be any different?

There are, of course, the infamous "Barnegat Pirates," a storied band of daring men who prowled the coastline in search of easy pickings from shipwrecks. "They do their share of stealin', I'll confess," said one alleged "pirate" to a Congressional Inquiry into Long Beach Island piracy, "but no man or woman was ever robbed on this beach till they was dead. It's innocent to what is done on Long Island. The Long Islanders cut off fingers of living people for rings, but the Barnegat men never touch the body till it's dead!"

Indeed, the first house built on the northern end of the island was said to be that of "Dad" Parker, who gained a reputation as a "Barnegat Pirate," in about 1800.

There are also the obligatory legends that purport to have a bit of Captain Kidd's treasure buried somewhere on Long Beach Island.

The probability of that being true is about equal to the probability that the Jersey Devil of the nearby Pine Barrens once trod the island sand — as it is rumored it did.

The most recurring and interesting pirate legend comes from the extreme southern end of the island, on what was once Tucker's Island.

Whether the "treasure" was that of a pirate's doing, and whether the finders and keepers of the loot were pirates themselves can only be debated in historical haze.

39

Tucker's Island was once a prosperous little place. There was a lighthouse, hotels, houses, a school and a Life Saving Station. The island faded completely from memory in the early 1930s, after being ravaged for decades by the sea.

It is well known that the area around Holgate has been rich with Spanish silver and gold coins. Around the turn of the century, such prizes by the hundreds were retrieved, especially following rough storms.

The legend of the Spanish coin treasure is placed sometime in the late part of the last century, and on or near what was Tucker's Island.

The men of the Life Saving Station on Tucker's Island were somewhat suspicious from the start when a sloop brought a pair of rugged mariners to its quiet front door. The two asked only two, but two very pointed questions. It seemed as if they may be up to no good.

Darkness was falling as they asked about the specific location of two notable cedar trees and an old lighthouse nearby. Their inquiries were handled courteously by the skeptical lifesaving crew, and they were thanked by the wayward seafarers for their help. The two men departed, saying they were settling down for the night.

A curious crew member followed the men visually from the tower of the station. He watched as they hastened to their boat, and returned to the beach with a load of what appeared to be shovels and tools.

The eavesdropping lifesaver lost sight of the pair as they disappeared into the darkness and beyond the dunes.

The lifesaver kept a vigil throughout the night, but at one point he dozed off for just a few moments. He was awakened by a stiff sea breeze and looked toward the surf where he spied the two men surreptitiously dragging a large "something" from the beach.

Believing the men's burden could have been anything from a body to stolen goods, the alert lifesaver sounded the alarm. Hearing that the Life Saving Station was coming alive with activity, the two men stepped up their mysterious activity.

The lifesaving crew rushed to the beach, but arrived just as the sailors were weighing anchor and setting sail. The crewmen, figuring they'd save their energies for whatever lifesaving duties might lay ahead, decided not to pursue the men.

They did pursue the root of the mystery, however. What brought the two men to the southern tip of Long Beach Island that dark evening? Why the interest in the two cedars and the old lighthouse? What were they carting away so stealthily?

The mystery started to unravel as pieces of evidence were gathered. The lifesavers started their probe at the two cedars, longtime landmarks of the island. Sure enough, between the trees was a gaping hole in the ground. Near it was an empty ironbound chest, a handful of Spanish coins, a tattered map, and a rusted cutlass.

How the men got the map, and what exactly was in the chest remain a mystery. The cutlass, though, is now the property of the Long Beach Island Historical Association, and can be seen at its museum.

# THE WRECK OF THE POWHATAN

Dark waves of Atlantic, all crested ,with white,
Were lifting their heads to the angel of night;
The south wind had lulled, the sky was o'ercast:
A sign when at sea to prepare for the blast.
The waves were in motion, toppling higher and higher,
And as they rolled on became tinged with fire —
An omen to sailors, when nearing the land
In cold, dreary winter, that a storm is at hand.
We were out on the sea very near to the coast,
In a staunch sailing vessel, the "Mariner's Boast."
We knew all the soundings and courses to steer,
The ledges and terrible breakers to clear.
Not so the Powhatan from o'er the main,
That's hove to and waiting a pilot to gain.
A true son of Neptune, that ship did command,
Freighted with souls from "Dear Father-land."
The hearts of the voyagers were joyous I ween,
As the lights on the land distinctly were seen;
Their land of adoption where kindred before
Had found an asylum on Liberty's shore.
Men with gray hairs, aged mothers were there,
Young husbands and wives, and all they held dear;
Gay youths and fair maidens, with eyes beaming love —
Those vows were recorded in heaven above.
O could we thus leave them, their voyage to complete,
As kind ones are waiting their faces to greet.
Our task would be ended, and we might forego

The pain of recording a sad tale of woe.
Four hundred souls were on shipboard that night,
When the storm burst upon them with terrible might.
It came like an avalanche sweeping before,
Driving the noble ship nearer the shore.
To picture the storm-fiend would baffle our pen;
We oftimes had fought him, but never like then.
The waves of Old Ocean mounted upward so high,
Their summits dissolved with the clouds of the sky;
While the winds rushing through mast, rigging and sail,
Resembled the sound of a loud, dying wail;
The sails of the ship into tatters were torn,
As shoreward she drifted, on rude billows borne —
While darkness o'erwhelmed them, she struck on a reef
Where no human soul could afford them relief.
When morning had banished the gloom of the night,
What a picture of woe to a lone wrecker's sight,
Who stood on a sandhill and viewed the sad scene
As surges swept past him through gorge and ravine.
Their cries of distress on the wings of the gale
From the lips of strong men, the fond mother's wail,
The shrieks of the maidens, the sound of despair,
As he tearfully gazed was borne on the air.
The bosum of Ocean was frightfully fed,
As wave after wave dashed over their head.
'Till a gigantic billow with deafening roar,
Broke the ship into atoms, driving fragments ashore.
O cold were the winds and chilling the blast
That blew as these souls on the rude beach were cast,
Torn, mangled and bleeding, yet gasping for breath,
Some alive reached the shore, but a terrible death
Awaited them there, for no human feet
Could traverse that sand-beach 'mid hail and sleet
And swelling surges that swept past the knolls,
At the brink of which perished very many poor souls.
O for a pen with a gift from above
The power to picture parental love —
A love that is left in the hour of despair

*Even stronger than death, was exhibited there.*
*Husbands and wives clasped together were found*
*When the storm had abated, strewn on the cold ground;*
*Even death had not vanquished loves lingering glow,*
*Or banished from bosoms the whiteness of snow;*
*Nor relaxed the strength of a fond parent's grasp,*
*Though a corpse, too, it was the child whom he clasped.*
*A hero was with them (but lost is his name)*
*Whose heart was undaunted — herculean his frame;*
*Neither ocean nor tempest then raging so wild,*
*Could banish affectionate care for his child —*
*With it locked in his arms through surges he'd flown,*
*Far up on the beach to where low shrubs had grown;*
*These up by the roots, like a giant he tore,*
*And built a rude shelter on that stormy shore,*
*To shield his dear infant — his last dying breath*
*Was breathed in its face, as over the Death*
*Threw his mantle — then angels above*
*Wafted their souls to the haven of love;*
*The child of his bosom, so fondly caressed,*
*With its arms 'round his neck was found on his breast.*
*Ye who have trodden on fields of the slain,*
*When co-mingled together in heaps they have lain*
*After the sulphurous war-cloud had fled,*
*Can picture the horrible scene of the dead.*
*Four hundred souls that Old Ocean had braved,*
*Perished and died, and not one was saved.*
*The home which they found in the long looked-for land,*
*Was a lowly grave dug by a stranger's hand.*

"Errick"
April, 1854

44

# THE HAUNTED MANSION

Any ghost story that entertains any hope at all of being credible should contain three basic and very important components: Fact, legend and personal experience.

First, there must be some element of fact — a verifiable episode or event that serves as the foundation for the second and third components.

The "legend" follows behind fact, and may often not manifest itself until much later than the factual event that sparked it.

The legend is built around the event, and creates the aura of mystery or speculation that can at once enhance and distort the details of the actual happening.

The final component, and perhaps the most important and elusive of the three, is the personal experience. This testimony, especially when compiled firsthand, can be the most spectacular and inspiring of all. Alas, it can also be the most devastating to the story as a whole.

Quite often, the folklorist, and more particularly the researcher of the supernatural faces the situation where one or even two of the components can be very strong and entirely believable, but the other or others are missing. This, then, can cast doubts upon the entire tale.

For example, a particular house, building or location can gain a reputation as being "haunted." This reputation can suffice to serve as the "legend" component. Everybody in the area will say it: "That place is haunted!" Ask them what they base that admonition upon, and they're hard pressed to provide a response. Ask them if anyone has ever professed to have "met" the "ghosts" there (personal experience) and they're equally at a loss to answer. "They say it's haunted" is their only reply. Unfortunately, this is not enough for the serious researcher.

Armed with this theory, you will detect even in this volume certain stories where a particular component is either missing or very weakly supported. That is precisely why this book carries the word "Legends" in its title.

The authors do not claim to be the judges and jurors of those who have provided the "personal experience" components of the supernatural stories herein. It is the responsibility of you, the reader, to determine the validity of each narrative. It is up to you to see if all elements are plugged in, and if all are accurate or strong enough to warrant your acceptance.

The following chapter typifies the classic "ghost story." The seaside setting, the "fact" that set the "legend" into motion, and a fascinating "personal experience" all contribute to a frightening story.

We shall turn the pages of time back to April 18, 1854. It is nearly dawn, the packet ship "Powhatan" is nearing the end of its long voyage from Rotterdam to New York. There are more than 300 passengers aboard, most wealthy German nationals seeking a new life under the beacon of Liberty's light.

The 29 crew members had catered well to the needs of the passengers and the demands of the sea. The journey aboard the 200-foot wooden schooner was relatively uneventful, at least as uneventful as a trip across the North Atlantic in April can be.

In the distance, toward the western horizon, the signs of the encroaching coastline could be discerned. Land birds were evident, and the experienced mariners could literally smell the land that was only a few miles away.

Captain Myers, the master of the Powhatan, sought safety from the brewing gales, and continued on a westerly course, eventually to hug the shore and assume a northerly route to Verrazano Narrows.

The storm raged on, developing into a full-blown blizzard. Wind and snow storms that late in the season can be particularly violent, and this particular one was to be among the most disastrous in the maritime history of Long Beach Island.

The ship was battened down for the worst, but even the most dour doomsayer could not have predicted the ultimate fate of the poor Powhatan that grim and grisly Sunday.

As the passengers huddled in their cabins and staterooms, warily riding out the maelstrom, the helmsman struggled valiantly against fate to stabilize the vessel.

Without warning, the wicked fist that is the shoals off Long Beach Island punched into the hull of the Powhatan, the first blow in a hopeless bout that would result in another knockout of another proud sailing ship.

Driving snow and wind all but obscured the view of the foundering ship from anyone on shore. Anyway, there were few souls on shore who could have witnessed the grounding of the Powhatan. These factors, as well as the reality that the closest thing to even resemble a primitive "lifesaving" station was Samuel Perrine's "House of Refuge" some five miles away at Harvey Cedars.

The ship smashed into the shoals as the day was breaking. The raging surf pounded and battered the hapless wreck, incessantly and indiscriminatingly tearing it apart with every surge.

Men, women, children — crewmen and passengers — were swept to their watery graves by the score. With their dying efforts, they scrambled in vain to save themselves. Many struggled into the rigging in a frantic but vain attempt to survive. The snow swirled, the wind whipped, and like small frozen birds, they dropped, one by one, from their lofty perches to their deaths. The waves pushed and drove the ship deeper into the sandy bottom, until it was some thirty feet down.

On shore, there was activity of both the sinister and survival kind. The distance to the nearest point of help, and the problems created by the violent weather would make any rescue attempt all but impossible. Volunteers alerted to the disaster scurried to organize and do whatever could be done.

As this hopeless activity was taking place on shore, the Powhatan and her 340 lives were being smothered by the sea. By early evening, April 18, 1854, the ship was ripped to shreds and there were no signs of life.

Bodies littered the surf and beach in a morbid scene. The storm, one of the most barbarous in the recorded history of the New Jersey coast, would not only spell doom for the Powhatan, but also the schooner "Manhattan," which ran aground within sight of the wreckage of the Powhatan just hours later. There was but one survivor of that wreck.

The loss of the Powhatan, her passengers and crew is the "fact" of this chapter. The second element, the "legend," began to take shape even before the corpses of the Powhatan victims would be buried.

The futile rescue and salvage attempts of the well-meaning men from Harvey Cedars have been overshadowed in the legend by the alleged dastardly deeds of one man who figures prominently in the formation of the ghost story.

Edward Jennings was virtually alone on the stretch of Long Beach Island then known as the "Great Swamp." That area later became more populated and was renamed Long Beach City. Today, it is Surf City.

At what is now the north side of West 7th Street, between Central and Barnegat Avenues, there stood a lonely building known in 1854 as the "Mansion of Health." In its day, it was a refuge from the burgeoning cities to the west and north, and in the long history of Long Beach Island, no single structure has been more associated with ghostly goings-on and haunted happenings than the Mansion of Health.

The mansion was opened in 1822 by a group of investors from Burlington, N.J. looking for more sumptuous accommodations than were available on Long Beach at the time. Standing three stories tall, with a tower atop its roof, this 120-foot long building, girdled by a broad porch all around it, was the largest hotel on the Jersey coast for many years. For more than three decades, it flourished with patronage by some of the wealthiest travelers around.

The balcony of the mansion ran the length of the top floor, providing a breathtaking view of the sea, a mere 500 feet away. The summer sea breezes were considered to have therapeutic qualities, and the rugged swales and swampland around the hotel had their own peculiar charms.

When it was started in 1821, the mansion was to supplement the smaller hostelries on the island. James Cranmer maintained a tavern at "Great Swamp." His wine cellar was constantly replenished by castoff ships' cargoes, and the finest products of the stills on the mainland added to Cranmer's respected stock. Farther down the island was Joseph Horner's boarding house, which later was expanded to become Bond's Long Beach House.

At five dollars a week, the cost of staying at the Mansion of Health was considered an outrage by some, but the mansion prospered.

The most important of the mansion's early proprietors was Hudson Buzby, and the hotel was often called "Buzby's Place." The small rooms often housed four or five persons, and accommodations were rather sparse. Still, men and women flocked to the mansion by the sea, to partake of Buzby's hospitality and the cleansing qualities of the seashore.

It is believed that the death knell was sounded for the Mansion of Health when, in 1847, the railroad from city to sea diverted from Long Beach Island and headed for Cape May. No longer was easy access to Long Beach Island a major drawing card. The rail line could speed folks from the Philadelphia area faster to the cape, and business on Long Beach Island started to wane, except perhaps for Bond's Hotel at Holgate.

After Buzby passed away, the mansion fell into the managerial hands of Edward Jennings. Little is known about Jennings, other than he and his family and a son-in-law lived in the mansion year-round, and was the designated man to file the official reports of any shipwrecks along a certain stretch of coast in his area. He was the Wreckmaster.

The "legend" and the "personal experience" of the story of the Haunted Mansion have both been furnished by the same individual. His name has been lost in time, and the few references to him in the annals of written history refer to him quite vaguely as "Captain Jim."

The captain remembered well the wreck of the Powhatan. "I was a youngster then," he told an interviewer in the early part of this century, "and I tell you, it was the awfullest sight I ever saw. Long rows of drowned people, all lying there with their white, still faces turned up to the sky. Some were women, with their dead babies clasped tight in their arms. Some were husbands and wives, whose bodies came ashore locked together in a death embrace. I'll never forget that sight as long as I live."

The old captain recalled that the officials and would-be rescuers didn't reach the wreck until the day after its demise. "By that time," he continued, "the bodies had all come ashore, and the wreckmaster had them all piled up on the sand. Well, the coroner came over and took charge. He began to inquire whether any money or valuables had been found, but the wreckmaster declared that not a solitary coin had been washed ashore. People thought that this was rather singular, as the emigrants were, most of them, well-to-do Germans, and were known to have brought a good deal of money with them, but it was concluded that it went down with the ship.

"Well, the poor emigrants were given pauper burial, and the people had begun to forget their suspicions until three or four months later there came another storm, and the sea broke clear over the beach, just below the Old Mansion, and washed away the sand. Next morning early two men from Manahawkin sailed across the bay and landed on the beach. They walked across the beach and one of them saw something curious close up against the stump of an old cedar tree. He called the other man's attention to it, and they went over to the stump. What they found was a pile of leather money-belts that would fill a wheelbarrow. Every one was cut open and empty. They had been buried in the sand close by the old stump, and the sea had washed away the covering."

There was no way it could be proven that Wreckmaster Edward Jennings robbed the bodies, but all fingers on the mainland pointed to him. His reputation shattered beyond repair, Jennings and family left the mansion and the state. Some say he made his way to the Deep South, where he established a sprawling plantation with many slaves. Others maintain that he went to the West Coast, to dabble in the gold rush.

Both versions of Jennings' fate dovetail when it was reported that Jennings met a just fate, murdered in a barroom brawl. It was also reported that his son-in-law, and presumed accomplice in the body-robbing on Long Beach Island, also died in a boating accident.

Whatever, the old captain continued: "After that, nobody lived in the Old Mansion for a long time. People would go there, stay a week or two and leave — and at last it was given up entirely to beach parties in the daytime, and ghosts at night.

Thus, the legend of the Haunted Mansion was born. Now, all that is left is the "personal experience." Again, we turn to the interview with Captain Jim.

"It was one August, about 1861," he said. "I was a young feller then, and with a half dozen more was over on the beach cutting salt hay. We didn't go home at nights, but did our own cooking in the Old Mansion kitchen, and at nights slept on piles of hay upstairs.

"We were a reckless lot of scamps, and reckoned that no ghosts could scare us. There was a big, full moon that night, and it was light as day. The muskeeters was pretty bad, too, and it was easier to stay awake than to go to sleep. Along toward midnight, me and two other fellers went out on the old balcony and began to race around the house. We hollered and yelled and chased each other for half an hour or so, and then we concluded we had better go to sleep, so we started for the window of the room where the rest were. The window was near one end of the ocean side, and as I came around the corner I stopped as if I had been shot, and my hair raised straight up on top of my head.

"Right there in front of that window stood a woman looking out over the sea, and in her arms she held a little child. I saw her as plain as I see you now. It seemed to me an hour that she stood there, but I don't suppose it was a second, and then she was gone.

"When I could move I looked around for the other boys, and they were standing there paralyzed. They had seen the woman, too. We didn't say much, and we didn't sleep much that night, and the next night we bunked out on the beach. The rest of the crowd made all manner of fun of us, but we had had all the ghost we wanted, and I never set foot inside the old house after that!"

The Mansion of Health burned down about ten years later, and on its site was built another hotel called the "Mansion House." A portion of Crane's in Surf City is made up of this later structure.

The old captain remembered the fire that destroyed the Mansion of Health: "A beach party had been roasting clams in the old oven, and in some way the fire got to the woodwork. It was as dry as tinder, and I hope the ghosts were all burnt up with it."

Still, as you pass by the site of the old mansion, beware — the restless spirits of the Powhatan victims may be right behind you!

# GHOST SHIPS OF BARNEGAT BAY

Perhaps nothing on the high seas is as eerie as the notion of a "ghost ship."

Throughout history, these phantoms of the fathoms have sailed the seas. Some are tattered and battered derelicts, devoid of crew and signs of life. Others, such as the legendary "Flying Dutchman," are more majestic, full-rigged vessels, sailing in and out of the imagination on the crests of bounding waves.

The waters on both sides of Long Beach Island have had their share of mystery craft, dubbed "ghost ships" out of sheer desperation by those who have seen them.

David Lee Martin, a Philadelphian who visits Long Beach Island every summer, recalled a frightening experience he and his girlfriend, Antoinette Durban, had on the sea about five miles off Beach Haven in the summer of 1983.

"Toni and I were in my father's boat, just for a ride down the coast. The seas were relatively light, maybe running two to four feet at the most. It was a little choppy in our 21-footer, but I sort of like it that way.

"You know, as I'm telling you this, it all comes back to me so vividly. It was really scary that day, and I still can't get used to telling somebody about what we saw because I think that they think that I'm crazy. You have to believe that I'm not!"

The young accountant appeared a bit uneasy as he shuffled in his chair and related his story.

"We weren't even fishing that day. We just went out for a joy cruise, I guess, to get away from it all for a few hours. As I remember, it was very overcast, but it really didn't look like there would be a storm in the near future. The weather radio said it would be just cloudy, with a 30 percent chance of rain.

"I know we were just off Beach Haven, and could easily see the land. There were a couple of boats nearby, but both of them were much farther in toward the shore. I remember Toni commenting that it looked like we had the whole ocean to ourselves.

"That turned out to be a very bad mis-statement. Just as she was saying it, I looked out over the port bow and saw a ship in the distance. It was probably only a couple of miles away, but it seemed to be wrapped in fog or something and also seemed to be much farther away. I have never really been a very good judge of distance.

"All I know is that the ship looked like something out of an old John Paul Jones movie or something. It was a typical sailing ship, a schooner or brig or something, and was square-rigged. I'm not really up on my types of old-time sailing ships. All I know is that I had never seen anything like it in the area before.

"I yelled to Toni, and I guess it scared her a little. I can't remember exactly what I said, but the thing really caught me off guard. I mean, I never, ever saw anything like it. Of course, I started to steer toward it, to take a closer look. It kept going in and out of the fog bank, and it was all very strange because there didn't seem to be any fog other than in the area around that ship.

"I really went full throttle toward the ship, but it seemed to keep its distance. Still, it looked like its bow was pointed toward us, as if it was headed our way. It really seemed strange that we didn't seem to be getting any closer.

"Toni went into the cabin for binoculars, and I tried to take a closer look. The waves were bobbing us up and down, though, and it was difficult to get a clear look.

"I know that Toni was fascinated by this mysterious ship, too. She kept staring at it and making jokes, like she always does. She said it was probably a British man-of-war, and we'd all be destroyed by her guns. She did a really bad Errol Flynn imitation, and made like we were about to go into battle. Then she hushed down and said it was more likely a pirate ship, and they'd come beside us, take all of our riches and kidnap her for ransom. This girl is a little strange, you know!

"While she was joking about it, I was really confused. I tried to make myself believe that it was just a regular sailing ship out of some other port, making her way up the coast. But I knew that there was something very odd about it all.

"Well, for about ten or twenty seconds, at the most, the fog around her seemed to lift. We seemed to be a little closer, and I could make out some details. It was still difficult to see, but I remember that the sails seemed to be really in bad shape — all torn and some flapping away in the breeze. There was a bright red stripe on her side, and no sign of anybody on board. Of course, it was still too far away to really make that determination.

"I won't swear to it, but I really think there was an anchor chain or rope going into the water from her bow. I thought that was very odd.

"As quickly as it lifted, though, the fog bank drifted back again. Then, then came the most frightening and confusing thing of all."

David shuffled in his seat again, and asked if he could take a couple of minutes off to get a glass of water. He returned, and continued his convincing story.

"I've got to tell you that this is very nerve-wracking for me. I only wish Toni was here to confirm all of this, but we're no longer seeing each other. I'd give you her last address if you want her to back me up.

"Anyway, as that fog bank rolled in again, the ship seemed to disappear for a second. Toni and I both looked at each other and neither of us was in a joking mood anymore. She asked me what I thought it was, and all I could do is shrug.

"We kept looking over to where the ship was, and saw nothing but fog. The ship seemed to be somewhere in the fog, but it became less and less visible.

"Then, the fog lifted again, and the area became almost perfectly clear. And you know what? That damned ship wasn't anywhere to be found! Toni gasped, and I shook my head. Now we were a little scared. It seemed like an hour until either of us said anything again. We were both very confused and frightened by it all.

"We debated whether or not to go toward where the ship was, and eventually decided not to. We thought our eyes might have been playing tricks on us, but we both knew better. What we saw was actually there, but had disappeared like, well, like a ghost ship!

"So, we brought the boat around and headed back to the inlet. We didn't know what to do or say, or if we should tell anybody about what we just saw. We decided that, probably, nobody would believe us anyhow. Other than our parents, who I don't think believed us, and a couple of close friends, you're the first person we — or I — have told."

Is there an explanation for what David and Toni saw that afternoon in the summer of 1983? Can it be explained rationally in some way?

These are the same questions asked by four people who had a somewhat similar experience nine or ten years ago, not on the high seas, but in the calm confines of Barnegat Bay.

We spoke to one of the quartet on the telephone, he speaking from his new home on the Florida Keys:

You do not want your name mentioned, is that correct?

CORRECT.

Give me a rundown of what you saw that day, if you will.

WHAT I FIRST SAW COMING TOWARD US WAS A BOWSPRIT WITH A CABLE RUNNING BACK UP TO THE BOAT. IT LOOKED LIKE THE BOW OF THE BOAT WAS OUT OF THE WATER ABOUT SIX OR SEVEN FEET. I SAW TWO MASTS WITH A LIGHT ON THE MAST UP HIGH.

Red, green or white light?

WHITE OR YELLOWISH, LIKE A LANTERN LIGHT. BUT IT WAS BRIGHT. I TURNED AWAY FROM

IT TO THROW MY LEFT ENGINE IN REVERSE, AND
FORWARD ON MY RIGHT ENGINE. THAT SWUNG
MY BOAT AROUND, THEN I BACKED OUT AWAY
FROM IT WITH BOTH THROTTLES WIDE OPEN.

Was it pretty close to you?

IT WAS PROBABLY 40 OR 50 FEET FROM ME.
THERE WERE BIG WAKES COMING OFF THE SIDE,
PROBABLY THREE FEET HIGH OR SO WITH BREAK-
ING WATER. AND WHEN I GOT OUT OF THE WAY,
AND AFTER ABOUT 2/3 OF THE BOAT WENT BY, I
SAW THE SECOND MAST CLEARLY, THE CABIN,
AND SOME PORTHOLES. I COULD SEE THE BOOM
BACK OVER THE SHIP FROM ONE OF THE MASTS
AND I COULD SEE THE WHEEL AT THE BACK DECK.

Could you see the sails?

I SAW THE WHITE SAILS.

Were they full?

YES, WHAT WIND THERE WAS THAT NIGHT WAS
COMING FROM BARNEGAT LIGHT.

About what time of year did you see this?

IN AUGUST OF '74 OR '75, AS BEST AS I CAN
REMEMBER NOW.

Was it a clear night?

CLEAR AS A BELL. STARS WERE SHINING.

No moon?

NO MOON.

You say there were four people on your boat?

FOUR PEOPLE ON THE BOAT. AND MY WIFE
DOESN'T DRINK. MY FRIEND'S WIFE DOESN'T
DRINK. THEY ALL SAW IT. THEY GOT EXCITED
BECAUSE THEY THOUGHT WE WERE GOING TO BE
RAMMED.

Have you ever had any other experiences?

NEVER.

Any other identifying marks on the boat?

THE ONLY THING, AS I GLANCED AT IT, IT HAD
A ROUND END. I PUT MY ENGINES FORWARD AND

TRIED TO FOLLOW IT, BUT IT WAS GONE. I COULDN'T BELIEVE IT. WITH MY BOAT I COULD DO 35 KNOTS.

What kind of boat did you have at the time?

I HAD A TWIN-ENGINE OWENS. 32 FOOT WATER LINE, 35 FOOT DECK.

Were you scared, in awe? What were your feelings?

AFTER I SAW THAT SHIP, I WAS SCARED. EVEN WHEN I TRIED TO FOLLOW IT. IT COULDN'T HAVE BEEN MORE THAN A HUNDRED FEET AHEAD OF ME WHEN I STARTED AFTER IT. I PULLED RIGHT OUT TO FOLLOW BEHIND IT.

I COULD SEE THE STARS AND EVERYTHING, BUT I COULDN'T SEE THE BOAT. I SAID "WHERE THE HELL DID THAT BOAT GO?" THE OTHERS SAID "I DON'T KNOW, MAYBE IT TURNED OFF. I SAID "I DON'T BELIEVE THIS." THAT BOAT HAD TO DRAW AT LEAST 12 TO 13 FEET OF WATER AND WE WERE ONLY IN 4 AND ONE-HALF FEET OF WATER. WE DECIDED RIGHT THERE TO STOP AND GET BACK TO THE DOCK. WE ALSO DECIDED TO NOT SAY A WORD TO ANYONE. THEY'D ALL THINK WE WERE NUTS. I WENT UP AND DOWN THE WATER THE NEXT DAY LOOKING FOR MASTS OR SOMETHING TO SHOW IF THERE WAS A BOAT THAT SIZE IN THE WATER OR IN THE AREA, JUST OUT OF CURIOSITY, THAT IT WOULD HAVE GONE AGROUND. WHEN I CHASED IT THAT NIGHT, I WOULD HAVE RAMMED IT IF IT WAS THERE. THERE WAS NO BOAT THERE.

Did you tell anyone about this?

I WAS AFRAID THEY WOULD LAUGH. THEY'D THINK I WAS NUTS.

Do you remember anything else about it?

I THINK I COULD DRAW A PICTURE OF IT, EVEN WITH ITS SAILS.

Was it square-rigged?

YES, IT HAD SQUARE SAILS. IT WAS AN OLD-TIME SAIL. NOW YOU DON'T SEE THEM ANYMORE.

YOU SEE MORE TRIANGULAR SAILS NOW.

The only light you saw was the one on the mast?

ON THE MAST. BUT IT LIGHTED UP THE WHOLE THING ON THE SIDE THAT PASSED US. IT DIDN'T LOOK LIKE A LANTERN LIGHT BECAUSE IT WAS YELLOWISH. IT LIGHTED UP THE WHOLE THING LIKE IT WAS YELLOW IN COLOR.

You didn't hear any sounds like the noise of an engine or people talking? Just the sound of the wake?

CORRECT.

What was your wife's and friends' opinion of it when they saw it?

THEY SAID RIGHT AWAY THAT IT HAD TO BE A GHOST SHIP.


The gentleman who once boated on Barnegat Bay but who has retired to Florida says he "didn't sleep for a week' following this mysterious encounter.

Could it be? Could there be a ghost ship sailing the vicinity of Long Beach Island? Did the imagination or atmospheric conditions play tricks on these unwilling witnesses to the unexplained?

There have been attempts to explain the phenomena. Perhaps the ghost ship is the Powhatan, doomed somehow to sail into eternity and haunt those who are unfortunate enough to come across her. As the ghosts of her pitiful crew and passengers are said to walk the beaches and towns of Long Beach Island, perhaps her hulk also roams the waters.

There are many more tales of ghost ships, some from as seemingly reliable sources as veteran fishermen and ancient reports from members of lifesaving crews. In all, they are simply more pieces of evidence that the legends of Long Beach Island continue to enrich the heritage of this land "six miles at sea."

# WORLD WAR II COMES
# TO LONG BEACH ISLAND

Although the word "legend" most often conjures up thoughts of deep, dark secrets that have emerged into popular lore from the deep, dark past, some legends actually are rooted in the not-too-distant memory.

Take, if you will, the growing legends surrounding the island's proximity to World War II, both in time and distance.

Many men and women who have their stories about the era are hesitant to talk. The memory is too vivid and painful, perhaps, or the stories are too simple and straightforward. Hardly, they believe, the stuff of legend.

It cannot be denied, though, that the war of the forties has spawned its own legends, sure to grow in intensity and proportion over the years.

From the petty chicanery of landbound thrill-seekers to the heroic actions of those who sailed the seas during these perilous times, the stories are only now beginning to surface.

"One thing I remember," recalls one lifelong island resident, "is the way the local boys used to get the goats of the Coast Guard patrolmen up at Barnegat Light.

"These patrolmen would walk up and down the beach at night, scouring the coast for lights, looking for any enemy submarines that might try to land personnel on the shore. Well, some local ne'er-do-wells would position themselves in the high sand dunes with 55-gallon steel drums they purloined somewhere. When a patrolman came near, they'd push the drums down the dunes, just to scare the hell out of the patrols. Usually, it worked. Then, the young men would scurry away, having gotten their kicks scaring these poor souls."

This same gent, who prefers to be anonymous, talks, too, of the night most of Barnegat Light and some of those on the mainland and down the island thought the Barnegat Inlet was under siege, or being invaded.

"I can't really remember exactly when during the war it was, but anybody who was on the island then can confirm that it really happened.

"As I recall, it was a quiet night, probably before or after the summertime. All of a sudden, a hellacious commotion broke out just north of the inlet. There were flashes of lights, lots of noise, and for a minute we really thought that we were under attack. We knew that German subs were reported to be cruising just off the shore, so there was always the uncertainty that they'd try something. As it turned out, though, that night the 'invasion' was simply an LST hugging the shore too closely, and ramming into the north jetty of Barnegat Inlet."

But yes, the war did come uncomfortably close to Long Beach Island. The iron and steel that litters the bottom of the sea a scant few milers off the beaches is mute testimony. The freighter TOLTEN was torpedoed on March 14, 1942, about 13 miles off Island Beach. The 4,900-ton Norwegian cargo vessel BIDEVENT went down with her 2,000 tons of manganese ore a month later.

The barge HARRY RUSE, now in some 95 feet of water, was lost 25 miles east of Beach Haven on February 17, 1942, presumably by a German torpedo. There are numerous other wrecks, charted and well-known, but still nameless and without any other information attached to them other than the presumption that they were victims of the enemy U-boats.

Actually, the submarines of the German navy first appeared off the coast of Long Beach in the first World War. As early as June 2, 1918, the first ship, the 1,778-ton schooner JACOB HASKELL, was reported sunk by the unterseeboots.

61

Most notable among the WWI U-boat victims are the SAN SABA and the CHAPARRA, both destroyed on October 1918 off Harvey Cedars. Both are described in more detail in the 1984 book, "Shipwrecks Near Barnegat Inlet."

The ships most often linked with action during the second world war are the GULFTRADE, PERSEPHONE and R.P. RESOR.

The 423-foot GULFTRADE, heading from Port Arthur, Texas, to New York, was northbound at about ten knots when taken by surprise by the Nazi sub. A torpedo ripped through her hull and split her in two. Her wreckage is spread over several miles. She was about 14 miles off the coast when struck by the fatal blow on March 10, 1942. Eighteen crewmen were killed when the ship burst into flames.

Two months later, May 15, 1942, the audacity of the Nazi submarine captains reached its peak when a scant two and one-half miles from Barnegat Light, well within sight of the lighthouse, the shoreline and "the land of the free," the unarmed tanker PERSEPHONE went down at the hands of the German sub.

"I was in my room," wrote Captain Helge Quistgaard of the PERSEPHONE in his report following the tragedy. "The weather was slightly hazy and the sea calm. Visibility was good. We were the last in a convoy, with ample protection both in the air and on the surface. At 2:58 p.m., a torpedo hit the ship on the starboard side in way of the engine room. A thick, black smoke covered the entire ship.

"About 45 seconds after the first explosion, another torpedo struck us at number eight tank, starboard side, causing large quantities of oil to spout onto the ship. The stern of the tanker settled immediately and rested on the bottom, leaving the bow and midship house sticking out of the water. I went to the bridge and gave orders to abandon ship.

"Number one lifeboat had been partly lowered by officers and crew who were amidship at the time of the torpedoing. It got safely away with seven men. I noticed that a large raft was already floating about 300 feet from the ship, with seventeen men on it. This raft was carried away by the back-

62

wash caused by the rapid settling of the ship's stern. A number of the crew, caught by the explosion as they were having coffee in the messroom, jumped onto this raft and were thus saved before it washed away.

"The Coast Guard vessel that picked us up gave chase to the sub, as did other escort units. At no time did the submarine show itself."

Captain Quistgaard's account provides a fine glimpse into the panic, and yet orderly salvation attempts, that struck the PERSEPHONE within seconds after the Nazi torpedo had done so. Nine men lost their lives that day.

More tragic in terms of human toll was the sinking of the Standard Oil tanker R.P. RESOR, which was sailing about 30 miles due east of the Barnegat Inlet on February 27, 1942, when she was victimized by yet another German submarine.

Sailing to Fall River, Mass. from Baytown, Texas, the RESOR passed by Long Beach Island just before midnight with her cargo of fuel oil.

What appeared to be the lights of a small fishing boat were tragically deceiving to the crew. As the men gazed at the distant lights, a torpedo rammed into the tanker's side and touched off an inferno. Several of the 47 men who died that night did so in that first blast.

It is not known what caused the second explosion some fifteen minutes later. The cargo could have gone up, or it could have been another underwater missile. Whatever, the second blow killed more and further damaged the ship. A Coast Guard patrol boat was quick to respond, but able only to save two men. The submarine was never spotted.

There have been other wartime losses, and accompanying stories about them. There are even the recurring rumors that the Germans actually did land spies on the shore of Long Beach Island, and these men managed to blend in with the populace and carry on their deeds of espionage from a base on the beautiful Jersey Shore. This has never been documented, and probably never can be.

# CONFESSIONS OF A BOOTLEGGER

One of the most infamous, and yet somehow intriguing, eras in the recent history of Long Beach Island was that of the Prohibition years of the 1920s and early 1930s. It was through the inlets and bays surrounding the island that innumerable cases of bootleg booze reached the eager palates on the mainland.

Many accounts of these "rum-runners" are locked forever in the still-secret minds of those involved. Only, perhaps, after an old fisherman or boat captain has had a bit too much of the product he once carted through Barnegat Bay will he divulge his involvement. Most, however, will die with their memories intact.

Most of the "rum-running" was done through Little Egg and Beach Haven inlets, although there is evidence that some of the hooch also passed through Barnegat Inlet. Very little liquor was landed on the island itself, but it was the island's watermen who served as the links between the sea-going supply ships and the waiting landlubbers.

One of those who piloted the illegal intoxicants through the bay was Herb Schoenberg, who speaks today with a strange kind of unabashed pride in his youthful endeavors.

"It was always done on certain nights of the month. Always before the holidays," says Schoenberg. "Weeks before the holiday, they'd start getting the crews ready.

"There were two concerns operating out of here — one from Atlantic City, run by the city's mayor — and the other from Newark. They hired mostly all local fellows on the beach, that is, to load a 55-foot speedboat that came from the mother ship and brought it into the inlet.

"From there, they were transferred to garveys. The garveys were 55 feet long, 11 and one-half feet wide, with underwater exhausts. Fully loaded, they only drew maybe two feet, and the underwater exhausts made them very quiet.

"Most all the liquor was brought in to the mainland, either from West Creek or on down to where Mystic Island is now. There's where it would be put on trucks and taken up to New York.

Most all the whiskey that came in here went either to Newark or New York."

Schoenberg's memory is fresh as it scans back a half-century and more. He recalls that there was no apparent link between the "gangs" operating in the central Jersey coast and the hard-core "Mafia" bootleggers.

"The whiskey that came through here all came from Canada. It was labeled 'Four Aces,' 'Guggenheim,' and was the finest kind of whiskey that could be bought. There was no moonshine, it was the real McCoy.

"They came in on fairly large sail vessels, smacks. The speed boats would unload from the mother ships and then the garveys would meet them at a certain spot. It was always at nighttime, and a lot of times the boats would run into trouble coming over the bar. They'd wind up with their propeller and shaft off. They'd have to dump the liquor overboard to avoid being caught red-handed. Then, the same gang that dumped the liquor would go out and retrieve it later on. But once the local people found out about a 'dump,' it was fair game."

The whiskey bottles were stuffed in hay and placed in burlap sacks. Brave boaters eager to beat the bootleggers at their own game would venture to the site of an aborted run, and use a grappler to retrieve the sacks from the bottom. Of course, anyone who did this ran the risk of being caught and having their boat confiscated.

Herb Schoenberg remembers a time when he and three friends were gunning for brants on Barnegat Bay when they came across a sack of Scotch floating in the water. They continued and found another, and another — a total of 13 cases of liquor unclaimed from a previous "dump."

There was no gangland rivalry evident during the bootlegging days, no gunplay, no movie-style intrigue. Yet, there were some close calls, and some incidents where the local runners wound up spending some time and money as the result of their adventures.

"One time," Schoenberg recalls, "there was a run made to a house on the oceanfront at Beach Haven Terrace. It was on Atlantic Avenue about four blocks north of where the Spray Beach Hotel is today. The house had a false cellar with a trap door.

"The Coast Guard patrolled up and down, from one station to another, and punched time clocks. As they passed a certain spot, the runners stopped bringing the liquor ashore, and as the Coast Guardsmen got up the beach a ways, they'd start up again.

"This one time, they were bringing the whiskey ashore, and the Coast Guard man either forgot to punch the clock, or met a girlfriend, or something. Anyway, they caught the fellows working the load. The captain of the Coast Guard station was called down to investigate, and as it turned out, the woman of the house with the false cellar knew nothing about what was going on, even though her son was right in the middle of it."

Herb claims that certain Coast Guard station officers were paid to overlook the activities of the nocturnal crews. "They were given a dollar a case for each shipment," he says. This knowledge proved profitable for Herb one summer a decade or more after the rum-running days.

Herb had his boat confiscated during World War II when the Coast Guard caught him navigating through a mine field, and in possession of a handgun and a camera. Herb had no malicious intent, but still the boat was taken to a boatyard. It was the middle of August, when all wooden boats must be given a coat of protective paint to prevent the hungry worms from doing their damage. Herb sought to have his boat taken out of impoundment long enough to give it a fresh coat of copper paint.

He went to the Coast Guard commandant in Philadelphia to plead his case. After climbing the chain of command, he finally spoke directly with the "top dog."

The commandant immediately recognized Herb's name, and quipped something like, "Hey, Schoenberg — weren't you one of those bad-boy rum-runners a few years back?"

"Yeah, that's me," Herb replied. When the commandant appeared a bit hesitant to grant Herb's wish, he added, ". . . and didn't you get your dollar a case back then?"

An embarrassed commandant quickly bailed out Herb's boat!

There was a time when Herb was not as quick on his feet, though, and through a bizarre chain of events wound up in the Atlantic City lockup for a spell.

Harkening thoughts again from the Prohibition years, Herb recalls a time when he went to retrieve a certain load of liquor that had been dumped earlier.

After dragging the shallow bottom, they managed to retrieve about two dozen bottles and loaded them onto the fishing boat. As they cruised back to port, a waiting Coast Guard boat spotted the grappler and ordered them to follow them.

As they made their way under Coast Guard observation, Herb managed to secrete the bottles in the pockets and lining of a set of double extra-large foul-weather gear. As the boat pulled into the dock, Herb hustled ashore, hoping that at worst, HE would be caught, but the boat's involvement could not be proven. He'd rather pay a fine than lose the boat.

As he walked away, the Coast Guardsmen ordered him to stop. He kept walking briskly, though, shouting that he was simply too cold to stop right then. He was transferred to a car for a ride to his fate at the Coast Guard station. As the car drove on, he quietly rolled down the back window, claiming he was too warm in the car, and managed to toss two bottles into high grass on the side of the road.

When they arrived at the Coast Guard station, his coat was still overloaded with bottles of booze. He was ordered to take off his coat, and the jig was up. He was taken to a federal magistrate in Atlantic City and fined $55 for smuggling 22 pints of liquor.

Herb had a half-hearted last laugh the next day, though. He retraced his car ride, and managed to find the two bottles he tossed out of the window. Grand retribution!

The rum-running days were exciting, to a degree, and profitable, to be sure. The crews were paid one hundred dollars per man per load, with an average load being 750 cases.

"The fellows who were involved always had a case of liquor at home, too," Herb says. They always made sure that a couple of cases were 'lost' during the night. There never was a full load brought to the dock.

Hotels and gathering spots on Long Beach Island were also stocked with the illegal liquor. The Acme Hotel and the "Antlers" were well-known as speakeasies, and the Beach Haven House and Hudson House were also havens for those who enjoyed a nip.

There is still a certain amount of fear or perhaps shame connected with some of those who ran the rum through the waters of Barnegat Bay. It is a shame that many of the stories locked within the hard and fast minds of those who choose not to talk will never reach the ears of those who wish to know more about this time in the life of Long Beach Island. But that's the way it is on this mysterious and marvelous strip of land.

# THE LONG BEACH MASSACRE

"I knew about the murders. I guess everybody does. But I don't think the knowledge that a few men were killed on that beach is what made me see what I saw that night. What I saw was real, and I'll never forget it."

The words are those of Clark Miller, a permanent resident of Newark, New Jersey, who spends as many as a dozen weekends a year at a friend's house in Barnegat Light.

Clark's story was not the easiest to obtain. "You're only about the second or third person I've told it to," the slender accountant assured the writer.

"I guess it's a matter of trying to avoid ridicule," he continued. "People who say they saw U.F.O.'s or ghosts always seem to be held in suspicion from that moment on. In fact, even I used to think that people who say they've experienced things like that were probably a little off their rockers. But ever since I saw those men that night, under those circumstances, I've changed my attitude."

Let us set the historical stage before Clark continues with his personal experience.

Sometime in the long ago, before beach houses peeked over the tops of the dunes and buoys winked and whistled off the breakers, the sands of Long Beach Island's beach was a desolate, foreboding place. A moonlit night provided the only illumination, and when clouds clutched the sky or the moon was new, the island was dark and uninviting.

More than likely, it was such a dark and dangerous night when the most heinous crime attached to a legend of Long

Beach Island played out on what is now the beach of Barnegat Light.

The incident has gained acceptance by historians, and eclipses the "legend" category. It has been deemed such a part of the New Jersey shore's history that it warrants its own historical marker, one of a precious few on Long Beach Island.

The American privateer ship, one of countless vessels that prowled the coast in a kind of gray area between pirate ship and Colonial support unit, was captained by Andrew Steel.

As the brig coasted perilously close to the Barnegat Shoals, her lookouts noticed another sailing ship dead in the water ahead. The mystery ship bore the cut of a British freighter.

Steel's ship, the "Alligator," went in for a closer look at the derelict. There was no sign of life, her sails were tattered and useless, and in Steel's arbitrary interpretation of the laws of the sea, the British cutter was fair game for salvage.

A search of the below decks showed that the abandoned ship's cargo belly was gorged with supplies.

The exact details of the evening's events have been peeled away by time. It is believed, however, that the load aboard the British ship was so large that the Alligator's crew needed help. That help was a bay away, in Waretown and Barnegat.

The hours passed as the men lifted the British cargo out of the holds and into the Alligator. So tedious was the work that more than two dozen of the men decided to row onto the shore for a good night's sleep on terra firma before continuing the backbreaking labor.

Unbeknownst to the men of the Alligator, a more ruthless pirate named John Bacon had ideas of his own about the laws of the sea.

Captain Bacon, who was the master of a band of buccaneers based on Island Beach, heard about the Alligator's find and was anxious to intrude on the Steel crew and claim a part of the booty as his own.

Island Beach, the spit of land to the north of Barnegat Inlet, was the rendezvous point for Bacon's ne'er-do-wells, and from there it was a short, silent row to the beach encampment of the Alligator crew.

In true pirate fashion, the cutthroats raided the slumbering salvagers and did away with them in a swift mass murder. Only five of the 26 men on the beach that night lived to tell their tales.

Today, only that historical marker (which, by the way, was missing from its pole at this writing) serves as a stark reminder of that barbarous event.

Or is it the ONLY reminder?

Clark Miller thinks not. Clark Miller says, with no doubt in his mind, no compromise in his voice, that there are ghosts on them thar dunes. Ghosts, he says, of the victims of the Long Beach Island Massacre!

"There's really not that much to my story," Clark says. "All I know is that it scared the hell out of me that one night, and nighttime on the beach has never been the same for me ever again.

"The sad thing about this is that I have no other witnesses to what happened that night. It would be easy for someone to say, well, I just made this up. But you've got to believe me that I didn't make it up, and I wasn't imagining it.

"The strange thing is, I never really gave the notion of ghosts much thought at all, ever. Like I said, I knew of the massacre because of the sign on the avenue. It always conjured up strange images in my mind, but ghosts weren't a part of it.

"Actually, the massacre and the history on that stretch of beach is what drew me there on several nights during the summer season I'd spend with my parents. They had a house down in Loveladies, but I always walked all the way up to the 7th or 8th Street beaches of Barnegat Light. The buoys and the breakers, boats going in and out of the inlet — all this was kind of romantic.

"Well, one night — I believe it was in early August —

last year, there was an incredibly bright moon, and things were really quiet at home. I told mom and dad I'd be going for a walk on the beach and headed out just after 9:30. Of course, I headed north to my favorite stretch of beach.

"I wasn't sure if it was full moon or not, but it certainly was bright. I walked out some street to the dunes, and came upon that mast that sticks out of the sand — the one you wrote about in your first book ("Shipwrecks Near Barnegat Inlet"). There was a roll of old snowfence or something just at the edge of the dunes, and I sat down for a while and just stared out to sea.

"I could see points of lights in the distance. I guess it was a ship in the shipping lanes or a fishing boat or whatever. A buoy with a red light was just a few hundred yards out, and I could hear the waves sloshing over the south jetty of the inlet. It may sound silly, but I really am touched by all of this. It sort of relaxes me.

"All kinds of thoughts went through my head. My job, my night school courses at college, my girlfriend and things like that. I was just relaxing and enjoying the last few days of the season. It all sort of recharged my batteries, you know.

"I was in a real peaceful frame of mind when I heard what sounded like a low moaning. It was almost like a growling dog, and something like the sound a dying person would make. It shook me up right away. I realized, though that it could be just about anything, and probably was something very easily explained. I don't know that I was actually frightened, but more confused as to what sound it was.

"This sound continued for a couple of minutes, and then I heard what sounded like the typical, low and deep chuckling you'd hear in a horror movie. It, too, was very soft, and barely recognizable over the sound of the surf. But I definitely heard it, and it was definitely human laughter.

"There really wasn't anyone near me at the time. Down the beach, I saw a few people walking along, and up around the bend, closer to the lighthouse, there were some others, but there wasn't anyone I could see within about a hundred yards of me. I stood up when I heard the laughing sound, and there was no one in back of me, either.

"The dunes right there are not as thick as just below. There really wasn't anyplace for somebody to hide to play a joke. I stayed as quiet as I could to see if I could hear anything else. In a few seconds, I realized that what I heard was only the beginning of a very weird experience.

"I looked down toward the ocean, toward that mast — the one you called the 'ghostly mast' in your shipwreck book — and saw a strange swirl of sand. It was like a little tornado or whirlpool. It was right at the edge of the water. That was the strangest thing about it, because right there the sand is wet and would not swirl up like that. But I saw it, and it was very clear under the bright moonlight.

"I watched it for maybe ten seconds until it seemed to take on a dull, greenish glow. You know, the first thing that came to my mind was an old movie I saw years ago. I think it was called 'The Fog' or something. It was about shipwreck victims who haunted an old lighthouse in Maine. It was like a scene out of that movie, but I never thought it would go so far as to be a shipwreck victim out to kill me.

"Luckily, I was right. But the swirl of sand continued to glow, getting brighter and dimmer from second to second. Eventually, it seemed to take the shape of a human being. You know, a smaller part, the head, on top. Broader shoulders, narrow at the legs. I guess it was partly my imagination, but it certainly appeared to have a human shape.

"I can't remember how I felt right then. I don't think I was scared even then, I really think I was just in awe of whatever was going on.

"After maybe a minute of watching this swirling sand, I heard the moaning sound again. This time, it was down toward the water, and was much louder. It was definitely the sound of a man in pain. By that time, I think I was frightened. Still, I stood there, just watching and listening.

"As the moaning sound got louder, another swirl of sand kicked up maybe five or six feet from the other one. Again, it started to glow and take on that shape. There was another moaning sound, and again that strange cackling laugh. I thought, am I going crazy? I looked around, and saw nobody nearby. I thought that maybe somebody else was close by, watching this strange thing, and we could talk to each other when it was all over to assure ourselves that it really took place. I was alone, though.

"Well, the whole episode took maybe two minutes. Those two minutes seemed like an hour, though. I just stood there, riveted to my spot on the dune, watching these two figures form in swirls of sand. The moaning continued to get louder, but not really loud. I squinted a bit to see if the shape was in any way recognizable, and thought of walking closer to the water, but something told me to stay right where I was.

"All of a sudden, at one flick of a second, there was a big splash in the surf and the moaning stopped. The swirls of sand disappeared, and everything was quiet. That splash sounded as if a fairly large boat or whale or something was dropped into the water in a bellyflop. It was very loud and kicked up a huge splash.

"I stood there amazed. Just what the hell did I see? What really bugged me is that I was alone. Who would believe me if I told them what I saw? Did I really see it? Was I asleep and dreaming? I knew I wasn't.

"That's all there really was to it. For me, though, it was enough. I still don't say that what I saw were ghosts, but how else can it be explained? It was certainly not natural, so I guess it had to be 'supernatural.' I guess whoever reads your book won't believe me, either. But I saw it, and heard it, just as I told you."

Clark Miller's attitude toward his experience is not unique. How does he rationalize what he experienced that lonely, moonlit night on a stretch of Long Beach Island where it is historically documented that the lives of more than twenty men were snuffed out by murderers?

If you dare, follow the next full moon to the "ghostly mast" of Barnegat Light and listen . . . listen closely. And most of all . . . beware!

74

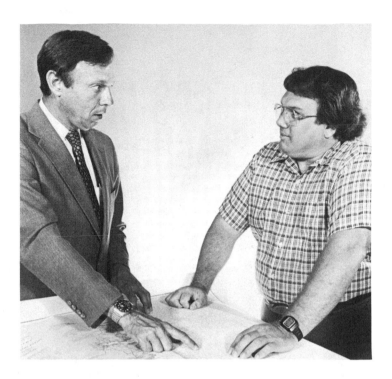

# ABOUT THE AUTHORS

Charles J. Adams III and David J. Seibold both live in the suburbs of Reading, Pa., and are both employed at radio station WEEU in that city.

Seibold also maintains a residence in Barnegat Light, N.J., and is an avid boater, fisherman and diver.

The two combined in 1984 to publish "Shipwrecks Near Barnegat Inlet," which went into a second printing in 1985.

Adams has written two books on ghost stories in his native Berks County, Pa., and writes regular travel and entertainment columns and features for the Reading EAGLE newspaper. He is a member of the Board of Trustees of the Reading Public Library, the Executive Council of the Historical Society of Berks County, and is on the board of directors of the Penn State Alumni Society of the Berks Campus.

Seibold is a former commodore of the Rajah Temple (Shrine) Yacht Club of Reading, and is a member of the Exchange Club of Hamburg, Pa., and the West Reading-Wyomissing Rotary Club.

LEGENDS OF
LONG BEACH ISLAND

PHOTO GALLERY

— THE OLD MANSION "LONG BEACH" —

THE HAUNTED MANSION — An early artist's rendering of the Mansion of Health, said to be haunted by the spirits of victims of the wreck of the packet steamer "Powhatan."

MASS BURIAL — After the "Powhatan" tragedy on Long Beach Island, cemeteries on the mainland were hard pressed for room to bury the victims. Many were interred in Manahawkin, while 54 corpses were carted by Isaac and Robert Smith of Smithville and buried in that village's Quaker Meeting House cemetery. The men of the congregation crafted coffins while the women stitched up burial garments. Later, several bodies were claimed, exhumed and re-buried in their native land. (BOTH PHOTOGRAPHS COURTESY DEB WHITCRAFT)

77

HADDOCK HOUSE — This early photo shows the John Haddock house in its original location in Barnegat Light.

HADDOCK HOUSE TODAY — After a series of storms at its original location near Barnegat Inlet, the Haddock house was moved to its present location on Long Beach Island Blvd. The ghosts of John Haddock and his wife are said to be seen on the widow's walk of the house. (BOTH PHOTOGRAPHS COURTESY OF RICHARD E. PLUNKETT, "WIZARD OF ODDS" ANTIQUE SHOP)

JOHN W. HADDOCK — This rare photograph captured Haddock in a playful mood as he (center) pets his dog. Haddock's spirit, it's believed, still occupies his Barnegat Light home. (PHOTO COURTESY RICHARD E. PLUNKETT)

HADDOCK'S GRAVE — The colorful John Haddock's instructions that he be buried in "Barnegat's Beam" were followed. His grave in a Waretown cemetery is on a small hill, and the Barnegat Lighthouse is visible from this vantage point.

MUTE TESTIMONY to the tragedies of the sea off Long Beach Island are tombstones such as these. In the foreground, a Swedish shipwreck victim was, as is on his marker, "buried by strangers." The monument in the background marks the resting place of unknown victims of the "Powhatan" disaster. The cemetery is in Manahawkin.

"HOMEWARD BOUND" — Cemeteries on the mainland are dotted with ornate tombstones such as this, marking the burials of victims of shipwrecks off Long Beach Island.

81

BARNEGAT
LIGHT-HOUSE.

"OLD BARNEY" — The historic Barnegat Lighthouse, on Long Beach Island's
northern tip, has stood guard there since the glory days of sail. Near its base, the
unmarked graves of unknown shipwreck victims harbor the bones of these hapless
sailors.

# The Sun-Set Hotel,

(FORMERLY SANS SOUCI,)

## BARNEGAT CITY, NEW JERSEY.

### RIDGWAY & BRADDOCK,
Proprietors.

THE SUN-SET HOTEL in Barnegat City (now Barnegat Light) was one of several large hotels on the island, destroyed by storm or neglect.

THE ELEGANCE of Bond's Long Beach House is evident in this artistic rendering of one of the island's all-time favorite hotels. (PHOTO COURTESY OF RICHARD E. PLUNKETT)

CO-AUTHOR DAVID J. SEIBOLD examines the inscription on a tombstone of a shipwreck victim in Manahawkin.

THE PERSEPHONE, an 8,400 ton tanker, seen in her prime. (PHOTO COUR-
TESY OF DEB WHITCRAFT)

THE R.P. RESOR — This Standard Oil tanker, like the Persephone, was
destroyed by a Nazi torpedo in World War II just a few miles from the Long Beach
Island shore. (PHOTO COURTESY OF DEB WHITCRAFT)

TWO DRAMATIC VIEWS of the tanker Persephone breaking apart and settling
on the bottom after being struck by a German U-Boat's torpedo on May 15, 1942.
(BOTH PHOTOS COURTESY OF DEB WHITCRAFT)

86

TWO VIEWS OF TWO APPROACHES to the aiding of shipwreck victims. In the top photo, a Navy dirigible passes over the mortally wounded Peresphone, sunk by Nazi torpedoes in 1942. In the lower cut, a ship in peril is approached by a speedy cutter in rough seas.